THREE-DOG NIGHT

GOURI DANGE is a writer and family counsellor based in Pune and Mumbai. This is her third novel and fifth book; she is a columnist with several national publications. Her abiding interest in the human struggle to change as well as the human resistance to change is seen in her writing, both fiction and non-fiction. A strong thread of humour – at times gentle and at times merciless – runs through her works. Music, dogs, the absurdities of city life, food (eating, cooking as well as growing it), cultures vastly different from ours are some of the other areas that she writes about.

THREE-DOG NIGHT

A Viva Voce Novel

Gouri Dange

HarperCollins *Publishers* India

First published in India in 2014 by
HarperCollins *Publishers* India

Building 10, Tower A, 4th Floor, DLF Cyber City, Phase II,
Gurugram Haryana – 122002, India
www.harpercollins.co.in

ISBN: 978-93-5136-151-0

2 4 6 8 10 9 7 5 3 1

Typeset in 11/14 Perpetua at
SURYA

Printed and bound at
MicroPrints India, New Delhi

Dedicated to
Annie, Snoopy, Yoyo, Jugnu, Bertie
and to all those who have loved them dearly

A word, a name, a sentence, a situation, a character, may ricochet in the mind of readers: familiar, startlingly like something seen or said or heard or done earlier. However, all characters, situations, and names in this work are fictitious; if they resemble anyone or any place, it only reconfirms the fact that there is a certain universality of human experience.

Also, this work is not autobiographical.

Contents

1

The Morning News

It was my young friend Moni, whispering urgently into the phone. Took me some seconds to figure out what she was saying because it was 5.20 in the morning, and I had jumped out of bed to answer the call thinking it was 'an emergency'. I forget that I'm almost sixty-one, and the elders for whom I might have had to run out in the night are gone. I'm more likely to become an emergency myself if I do this kind of leap without giving my feet and ankles prior notice.

So when I heard Moni whispering, 'Viva, listen, he finally spent the whole night here,' I wanted to bop her on the head.

She was talking about the creep that she had been seeing for over a year now. Why a free man aged forty-two seeing a free woman of forty-one would behave so furtive about being with her – like he was cheating on his wife or involved with a minor girl – is something I had not understood. Anyway, so *he stayed all night* was Moni's big dawn-breaking news and, well, I should be happy for her if this was really some kind of milestone in her deal with this feckless fellow. 'Commitment-phobic' they are grandly called now. Cad is what my father's gen would have called him. 'Swine' is what I muttered in my head.

She whispered on, 'Only thing is, he asked me if I had any lingerie that I could wear for him, and I didn't have any of that high-end stuff . . . but Viva . . .' and here a small giggle escaped her, '. . . he said, "you got the bod for it babe, why don't you get yourself some lingerie".' Her verbatim almost reverential repeating of this throwaway sentence from the man was annoying and sad in equal parts.

Listening to my silence, Moni said softly, 'Sorry Viva, if this is way too much information for you.'

No it is not too much information for me, because your generation didn't invent sex and allied lingerie, and I have a fair idea of how it works, so it is not too much information for me, I wanted to say. The other point is, if I remember right, men who fancied seeing a woman in lingerie *got* her that lingerie – they didn't point her to the lingerie store, for god's sake. Really, what a passive stingy stinker this guy sounds like. And here was Moni burbling on like she had just got advance inside information about being bestowed a Padmashri on Republic Day.

All I said, though, was, 'And did he pronounce it linggeree?'

'This is not the time to trash him, Viva, please,' Moni's voice remained low but urgently pleading.

Yes, I really should stop that. Likely to make Moni feel protective about him. And it did mean something, maybe, that El Creepo had stayed over, in spite of his mummy's midnight curfew. (You're sure you're not seeing Cinderella in man's clothing, no? I had once asked Moni. And the silly thing had repeated my remark to him, so of course he didn't like me at all, before we had even met. Very mutual.)

But the thought of this otherwise bright, well-adjusted and lovely woman being strung along and treated like a guilty secret made me even angrier with her than with this yucko that she was seeing. Most of her friends were done with asking her what she was doing with someone who would not even publicly acknowledge her as a girlfriend. And that's probably why she had only me to call up. Or perhaps she was calling other friends too with her feverishly whispered good news, poor kid.

'Okay, okay,' I said, trying to sound enthusiastic, or at least not-impatient. 'Now tell him to take you out for breakfast and then lingerie shopping later,' and watch him flee the spot the minute you suggest it, is what I didn't add. Anyway, Moni didn't want my gloomy prognostications right now; she just wanted some sort of permission to hope. And why was I fastidiously insisting on reality?

'Okaybyeheswokenup,' she said and went off the phone.

There was no point going back to bed now. The Mumbai crows had started up, shouting out their claims over the garbage pickings. The daft pigeons on my window ledge had begun their gormless activities, like going round and round in small circles, cooing and laying eggs on the smooth flat top of the air conditioner so that they rolled off and splattered sunny side up on the ledge below. How they managed to pass on their fine genes in this way, I don't know, but the pigeon population was definitely not dwindling. I don't know if I imagine this, but the much smarter bulbul on the jamun branch seems to spend a lot of time eyeing the pigeons and their dumbcluck ways, looking quite disapproving. Really. He or she looks sharply from them to me . . . as if to say, 'Did you see that? Can you believe these people?' and sometimes even gives a little impatient flick of the head before flying off purposefully.

I climb into my track pants and on to my exercycle. 'Exercise even before teeth, tea and tatti' had been Ashwin's motto, which I had never followed over our thirty-six years. Over the last eighteen months though, with him gone, I found that it had become my motto. Teeth-tea-tatti, I would murmur under my breath, like him. Earlier, I would let the tears flow while I cycled furiously; in the last few months, the tears had stopped.

The first few weeks after Ashwin's passing away, I would wake up and feel like a smudge of toothpaste that had just come out of the tube and missed the toothbrush; can't go back inside the tube, and the only option is to sit pointlessly in the washbasin and then go sadly down the drain.

But I didn't feel that way anymore. All the clichés about grieving and healing are true. Life does go on.

Except, of course, for a couple of people from my life with Ashwin, who will swoop down on me and instantly cry and hug me for far too long on a sweaty Mumbai street, or come up to me and incline their heads slightly to indicate deep sympathy and ask in a low murmur: How *are* you Vibhavari? or *How* are you Vibhavari? or How are *you* Vibhavari? For some reason, always the long version of my name. To add gravitas and solemnity, I suppose. I'm sure when they unclasp me and go their way, and meet someone, they say grimly, 'I met Vibhavari Pradhan today'. I'm sure there will be appropriate clucks and nods.

Call me an ungracious cow, but I have a theory that some of these wives of Ashwin's colleagues need to keep me on the Poor Vibhavari pedestal, so that the slot is taken and Misfortune doesn't look for another victim too close by. I'm their lightning conductor.

My exercycle showed a full twenty-six minutes. Anything under half an hour, and Ashwin would throw his well-worn joke at me, 'bike got a flat tyre?' Recently, I'd managed to get past the fifteen-minute mark without looking again and again at the meter. And that too without watching re-runs of *Friends* while I was cycling. Watching TV ensured that I didn't have to chaavi myself by imagining all kinds of dire health consequences if I stopped pedaling. But now some spoilsport had told me that watching TV and exercising at the same time was begging for retinal dislocation. Oh well.

I hate that growing old seems to be this see-saw act where you have to constantly take an either/or call on things like whether to keep that TV on so that you stay on that exercyle, or save your eyes but exercise half-heartedly. And after all that careful consideration, you can still end up getting brittle bones and go blind too. It's like when we were kids and offered the choice of 'milk-with-raw egg or extra arithmetic sums?' You sweated the choice and then squared your shoulders and opted to drink up the yech-milk. And then you found that, by some clever adult's sleight-of-hand, you ended up having to do the extra sums too, a little later, with the taste of raw egg still on your lips.

2

An Audience of One

Moni hadn't called after that; it was almost four days since her 'he stayed all night' milestone. And I wondered if it was a good thing or a bad thing that she hadn't called. Or maybe she just got busy with other things besides Shishir (who I called Chichi in my head). But I had nicer things to think of.

Dhruvi was coming today from Pune. Thirteen years ago, this creature and I had set eyes on each other in a neo-natal critical care ambulance, when his mother, my son's wife, had to be delivered of him far too early, at just twenty-eight weeks. Toxemia, it is called. One of those 'it happens' medical things. No real known reason or explanation why.

The doctors had hurried into the OT, saying to us grimly at the door in doctorspeak, 'Our priority is the mother'. That translates in humanspeak to 'the baby is a goner'. But ten minutes later, there they were, the same two doctors, grinning under their masks, I swear almost giggling, at the doorway. 'We have an active baby here' they said, and beckoned that baby's two grandmothers in for a very quick peek before he was put into tube-and-glass-bubble land.

Such unalloyed joy on the faces of doctors who must have delivered thousands of babies up to now, dead and alive, made me want to hug them, but one of them quickly went back into robot-doctor-mode and said in an R2D2 voice that effectively deterred any public-display-of-affection, 'Someone will have to accompany Baby in the ambulance.' At which point, the other new-grandma blacked out and fell gently against me, all exhausted eighty-nine kgs of her. My son, ashen-faced, was inside with his wife. My husband was away in Malaysia, and so there I was, usually so squeamish about hospitals and doctors, now jumping into the ambulance, jelly-legs and all.

The ambulance was to take the baby from one part of the hospital premises to another part of it, across a road and six flights up to the neo-natal critical care place. This involved the vehicle taking a left turn out of the gate on to a busy Mumbai road, merging with traffic to the right, and then negotiating a U-turn to go to the opposite side of the road.

There were three youngsters inside the ambulance – doctor, nurse and attendant – sitting in a huddle around the glass case in which the baby was, and they were fully focused on the struggling new being. I had gotten used to most young people jabbering all the time (jabbing at cell phones had not yet become a national passion thirteen years ago), and the sight of these three people's quiet, almost reverential attention to holding the tubes and things in place made the blood in my body surge with a mix of pride (the mera bharat mahan kind) and gratitude.

This is when Dhruvi and I looked at each other; I know babies that little can't see as such, but he seemed to be looking straight at me. And he was almost hollering – not in an abject reedy voice, as you may expect from a 900 gm preemie, but in a pissed-off-with-this-sudden-change-of-plans way – and I laughed out loud and wept. The ambulance, in spite of the light and siren, was not being able to move ahead fast enough. I managed to shout out to the man in a green car on the left side who would not give way to us: '*Ay gadhe-ki-aulad, baju ho ja, sunai-dikhai nahi deta kya*, moron?' The ambulance driver and the accompanying staff just nodded their heads hopelessly – they must have seen this kind of non-yielding of traffic too many times to be surprised or angry.

So the first words that hit my grandson's ears were his grandmom cussing, I'm afraid. Not at all how it was planned for him. My son and daughter-in-law had specifically planned to have a string of Malhars playing softly right through the birthing because the baby was expected in rainy July, and they wanted him to be born to the sounds of monsoon ragas. They had the sequence ready on a CD – starting with a *Megh Malhar*, then a *Miya*, and on to a *Gaud* and others and ending in *Jayant Malhar*. But an ambulance siren and gaali-galoch and the Mumbai road roar is what first fell on his ears.

As we all tumbled out of the ambulance on arrival and went up the lift of the neo-natal section, the nurse asked me, 'Baby ka maasi?' I was almost forty-nine years old at the time and should have been flattered, but I think it was more the gaali-giving – rather than youthful looks – that made me appear non-grandmom material.

He struggled through his first six weeks, and came out most okay. This sole grandson of mine and I have been buddies ever since. And the buddiness changes subtly and suitably as he grows up and I grow old. With my husband Ashwin gone, there's a whole lot of guy stuff that Dhruvi doesn't get to do in Mumbai (like puttering around in Lohar Chawl and buying baffling looking tools that I never actually saw being used in the house except on that one day that they were bought).

His school near Pune is some new-fangled new-agey joint, which has holidays when no other soul his age has vacations. When he wants to visit me, his parents put him on a train or a bus, and he simply shows up at my door, hopping on to a BEST bus that he loves so much, for the last stretch. He insists, since he turned twelve, that he does it himself and will not be picked up from the station. Fortunately, his Ma is not the sort who'd give him a cell phone on which she can check when he breathed in and when he breathed out all the way from Pune to Mumbai. And she doesn't call me and hyperventilate till she gets that 'he's reached' SMS from me.

Today Dhruvi rings my doorbell in a grown-up and considerate little bing-bong, and I walk quickly to the door. This is one of the ways he and I have grown older. Earlier it would be an exuberant bingbongbingbongbing and I would tumble over stuff to run to get the door, with Ashwin muttering 'slow down, slow down'.

When people talk about uncaring, sullen and self-absorbed grandchildren, I can't join in even just to pretend that I belong. (Now if the topic was about sullen self-absorbed daughters, however, sure I could contribute quite meaningfully to the discussion. My daughter is a card-carrying member of *that* club.)

He has become a rich walnut-brown from his swimming. We hug, he murmurs 'Viyaa Viyaa' and I say 'My Dhruvlet'.

My cell phone rang – it's that time of day, when I get phone calls from people selling things. My phone company has me on some 'no-solicitation-calls' mode, but obviously their filter has big holes in it, or the mode comes unstuck periodically, who knows. I took the unknown-number call, with an exaggeratedly cheerful and welcoming 'Yeeess?' just for fun.

Dhruv grinned, and picked up one from the plate of big fat potato-mince patties that I had got him. I pulled out the giant glass of sitaphal milkshake from the fridge for him as I waited for the caller to speak up. Of course it was a telemarketer on the phone. Usually I would have said 'no thank you' as soon as the caller began her spiel. But this one, I wanted to speak to.

First a brief backgrounder: last week I got one of those 'pre-approved' credit cards in my mail – complete with my name embossed on it – from a bank with whom I have never banked or transacted any business. It came with the usual glossy colourful brochures, which I promptly cut up into little squares and gave to Farhaan the paper-mosaic artist who lives on the ground floor. As for the card, I cut it into four pieces with my kitchen scissors, put it in the bank's postage pre-paid envelope, and mailed it right back to them. It was my wordless 'no, thank you' – a little social grace taught to me recently by a friend who got about three of these in the mail every week at one time. Earlier, I would have spent my life-breath trying to call the bank and get an actual person at the other end and ask them why the heck they had sent me the card and how could I cancel it immediately, and all that earnest stuff. This returning a cut-up card was a deliciously wordless retort. I loved it.

But somehow, the bank seemed to have not got my subtle hint. So here was a Miss Shweta calling from this bank and asking, 'Ma'am, you have not used your card yet, you are aware you have to use it once to activate fully and avail of this facility, yes Ma'am?'

Now, normally I would have said something like, 'Shweta, child, when I send you a card cut into four, does that look like I want to avail of your facility?'

However, I simply said, 'No, thank you.'

To which she asked, 'May I know the reason why?'

Again, on an ordinary day, I would have been tempted to say 'No you may not', or descended into some childish retort like 'Because the sky is so high, that's why'.

But I found myself saying, thinking this up on the spot, 'Because our cult doesn't use credit cards. I don't use money either. I use the barter system.' Dhruv looked up mid-bite, as he was wolfing down his second keema patty, and grinned; his eyes lit up.

3

Coffee and Kanjeevarams

Dhruv had refilled his sitaphal milk shake glass and was back at the table grinning, and mouthed silently, 'barter?'

Poor Shweta the telemarketer. I could hear her gulping, and then she said, 'Ibegyourpardonma'am?'

I said, 'We use no cash, only barter. B-a-r-t-e-r: b for Bombay, a for Asia, r for Ratnagiri, t for telephone, e for elephant, r for Ratnagiri . . . Barter. Exchange of goods and services. We don't use cash or credit at all.' And for good measure I added, 'We are a cult.'

I had put her on speakerphone. Dhruv let out a muffled guffaw. I began to totally play to the galleries. My one-boy audience!

In a slightly faint voice, she asked, 'Ma'am what is the nature of your work?'

A series of lovely lies floated into my head, but I told her the truth, which was pretty confusing for Ms Shweta anyway, 'I photograph street dogs, galli-kuttas, I am photographer to the dogs of Mumbai.'

She could not compute that, so she went on to her next question.

'But ma'am you need a card or cash no? When you need to buy things . . . groceries, white goods, etc?' she asked hopefully.

'No. The people I work for pay me in dalia sacks – cracked wheat, you know,' I volunteered, and offered her an extra nugget of info, that I ate dalia for breakfast.

While she was digesting this dalia-sack reply, I added, 'And some clients pay me in fruits and vegetables. For particularly challenging assignments, they pay me with microwaves, hair dryers. Recently for a large project I got paid with a small car. So you see, I don't need to buy or sell anything with money or credit.'

At this point, Shweta went dead silent for a few seconds, said faintly, 'One minute ma'am' and passed the phone to one Rahul who said smoothly, 'Rahul this side ma'am, I believe you are looking for a car loan?'

I said, 'No, no . . . Rahul-beta, I just said that I wanted to exchange my car for fifteen sacks of dalia or a holiday to Europe. You in the market for it, Rahul?'

Now Dhruvi got up and ran out of the room spluttering his sitaphal milkshake, but staying within earshot.

Rahul-this-side-ma'am, mustering up all the dignity and presence of mind taught to him at home and in B-school, said, 'Ma'am please speak to our Area Manager.'

And then came Neha-here. To whom I said, 'You know, Neha, credit-shedit, loans-woans . . . all these are going out of fashion. You must re-train your people in BEG. It's the next big thing in the consumer finance sector. And I'm a BEG Consultant.'

'I beg your pardon?' Neha asked, now deeply confused.

Dhruv was howling with laughter now at the far end of my apartment.

'B-E-G – Barter and Exchange of Goods,' I told her patiently. 'It's a completely new way for the economy to function. Actually it's how our ancestors transacted business. And now it's a subject being offered in all the big B-schools. You can call me to your bank any time as a consultant on BEG. All I will ask for in exchange is thirty floor tiles to re-do my bathroom.'

At which point, she disconnected the call. I had achieved the hitherto unachievable: getting this kind of telemarketer to get off the phone before I did.

It was such fun at last to not yell and be exasperated and say sarcastic things or slam the phone down or pretend that I was the maid and shout into the phone, '*Didi ghar mey nahi hai, baad mey phone karo.*'

Dhruv romped back into the room, laughing out loud. 'Oh Viyaa . . . you ragged them, like college ragging . . .' he said, wiping off a milkshake moustache.

It was time to do some work now. I opened my clothes cupboard and Dhruv looked over my shoulder. He was one of the few people who approved of the wardrobe-culling scheme that I had embarked on. All the natty dressing of my Ashwin & Viva years now seemed like just too much fiddle-fuss to me. I was giving it away in small bunches, to anyone who wanted scarves and trinkets and sandals and make-up and saris and dupattas and perfumes and all that jazz. My aim was to bring it all down to five trousers and ten shirts/kurtis. And perhaps one kajal-stick and one lipstick called Plum Paradise or some such.

Why didn't I just give it all away in one fell-swoop? Well, it was a mixed thing for me. Giving it away did mean that I could be done with my least favourite aspect of being Mrs Pradhan – which had been dressing up at least twice a week and hobnobbing with Ashwin's colleagues, many of whom were horribly snooty corporate women who barely gave you the time of day because you were a stay-at-home mommy at the time. Or then there was that other bunch of women at these parties, who so loved being Mrs So-and-so, and dressing up and plotting what acquisition they would wheedle out of their Mr So-and-so.

But giving away that stuff also reminded me of some of our conversations, as we planned the retirement years, Ashwin and I. 'You can go junglee, Viva,' he would say, when we talked about moving out of Mumbai, and building a house and offering a home-stay thingy in the Sahyadri hills. I know how much he liked me to be well turned-out, but he knew how much happier I would be in a random trouser and a random shirt and living in a random spot in the world.

Now, going junglee without Ashwin seemed like a sad, silly and slightly scary thing to do.

And then there was my daughter, Shruti. Should I offer her first-dibs on the stuff I was giving away and then put up with Shruti being her contrary, sullen, accusatory self? There, I've said it, about my own flesh and blood, but what to do, it's like that between her and me and has been since she was seventeen. I'm not proud of it, but I'm not going to cover either for her or myself any more.

So offering Shruti my things could mean that she slopes into the house (she doesn't live with me) and says things that go something like this: 'You're giving *this* away? Baba got it for you from Dhaka.' Or then quite the opposite: 'Do you even *know* me? Why would I want this?' or then later: 'Why didn't you ask me before just giving it off to just anybody. I *wanted* that sari.' Or sometimes just a shrug and a twisted smile, which would leave me guessing whether she meant 'do-what-you-like' or 'anyway-you-always-do-what-you-like'.

Was I actually scared of Shruti, now that there was no Ashwin between her and me, and my son had sort of given up on her? I wondered sometimes. A couple of friends had asked me outright – why are you afraid of Shruti?

I wasn't scared, but yes, this thirty-four-year-old child of mine, I now dealt with with a mixture of appeasement and avoidance. But more on how this came to be, later.

I flipped through the row of sari-hangers today. I picked off the black-coffee/milky-coffee combo Kanjeevaram silk from its hanger. Ashwin had bought it for me ages ago after I had thought up a coffee-cream dessert that he had loved. I called it Coffee Crystal and Dhruv called it Pears-soap Pudding. It had that kind of dreamy pellucid colour that you could see because I set it in transparent demitasse cups or brandy glasses.

Perhaps I would make it today, and call Moni for a nightcap, and then give her the sari. She would look most lovely in it on some suitable occasion. Dhruv had never tasted my Coffee Crystal because there was alcohol in it. Perhaps today I would give him a little spoon of it. So I called up Moni and she promised to come over. I didn't tell her about the Kanjeevaram sari, just about dessert and about Dhruv being there.

We decided to make it together, Dhruv and I. You can't really call it a dessert. It's a double-entendre nightcap really. The coffee and demerara sugar in it wires you up for a range of post-dinner activities, from the routine to the sublime. The alcohol in it works from the opposite direction, warding off the threat of coffee-induced insomnia. Ashwin would whisper menacingly, Ajit-boss style, 'coffee sonay nahi degiii, aur daru jaagnay nahi degaaah.'

Here's how you make a cup of my Coffee Crystal.

Multiply the recipe for more:

Get started about 4 hours before you serve it; not very much later (it might not set) or earlier (it might over-set into a slightly flubbery version)

1 small cup water heated just below boiling point

add 1 heaped teaspoon strong instant coffee

add 2 heaped teaspoons demerara (brown) sugar

add 1 level teaspoon gelatine

stir well till everything's dissolved

pass through a tea-strainer to eliminate any bits of gelatine stubbornly floating around.

mix in a chota-peg of brandy/whisky. Any kind. You got cognac or malt to spare, throw it in. You got plain old Indian stuff, it works as well.

pour this liquid, while still warm, into a goblet or a transparent coffee cup

place in fridge where it won't get jostled too much
about three hours later, it will have set
now pour a couple of tablespoons of whipped cream over it
dust lightly with cinnamon or cocoa powder.
Instead of cream, you could lay on some Bailey's Irish Cream over the set coffee.

4

Karaoke Knight

As Moni polished off her second cup of the Coffee Crystal, allowing Dhruv a second spoonful, I went into my room and brought out the Kanjeevaram sari, which I had wrapped in an old scarf for her.

Her soft black eyes widened. 'No! Not this one, Viva? You can't give away this one, even to me . . .' she said. But she rose and held it against herself and twirled in front of my mirror, looking quite like a swirl of coffee-and-cream herself.

'Tell you what,' she said in a rush. 'Shishir has called me and some friends to a karaoke evening at a Manna Dey fan club thing where he's going to sing on Friday. I'll wear this gorgeous sari and we'll go together, yah? Dhruvi don't yawn. It will be great fun, promise.'

I was not that sure I wanted to go out for a whole evening with this Chichi Shishir of hers. And about listening to karaoke singers slaughter old songs, I was even less enthusiastic. But I would not be able to duck the inevitable anymore – Moni was keen that we meet, especially since the blighter seemed to be 'staying the night' once in a while now in her life. So I said yes. Dhruv had the grace and wisdom (seriously, at thirteen he did, and I'm not just being a fawning-foolish fan grandma here) to not protest. He said 'sure' (the total opposite of 'whatever'). Moni was on the phone at once, telling Shishir that she had invited us to his karaoke night.

She folded and wrapped up the sari carefully. In the hallway outside my door, I stood with her waiting for the lift; when the doors opened she gave me a hug and said in a rush, 'Are you sure about the sari–thanks–I'm going before you change your mind'. I managed to say, 'You know how pleased Ashwin would have been that I gave it to you, Moni.' And the doors shut and she was gone.

On Friday, we picked her up from her office, where she had changed into the coffee sari. She looked most lovely, like I thought she would. Even Dhruvi said so (a quick shy look at her and a 'cool'; he was not old enough yet to say 'hot').

I could see a hint of brown eye make-up and a near-nude lipstick. Moni's bright mobile face was doing its best to stay composed and elegant. She had done something parlourish to her hair and it fell softly about her shoulders, released from the usual knot that she wore. The slightly awkward walk because she wasn't much used to saris looked charming in its own way too, I thought, as she hurried to the car.

As she got in and settled herself and her sari with unaccustomed care, she said, 'He's called two of his friends from work too.'

Most likely this too was a big one for Moni – that the man was now vaguely ready to Introduce her to His Friends.

The extreme show of casualness and nonchalance with which even people in their forties have to conduct the initiation of a relationship is one of the (many) things about which I feel 'thank god it was not that way in our times'.

When we reached, Shishir was waiting at the entrance of the club. So this was the successful graphic artist bloke that Moni was so full of hope about. He was shortish, balding, fair, a bit portly, dressed in an expensive-looking shirt and trousers. He had a self-important manner that may have become a bit exaggerated because he was meeting me for the first time and was aware that I didn't like how he was being with Moni, perhaps. Or maybe it was because he was going to sing on stage.

He took us in and seated us with two of his friends who seemed somehow nicer than him, and I wondered idly and pointlessly why Moni couldn't have found a good man like one of these. Anyway, our drinks arrived and the list of amateur singers in the karaoke competition was being announced. A beautifully done charcoal sketch of Manna Dey was the backdrop to the stage.

We sat in a kind of semi-circle at our round table with our drinks and finger foods in front of us. Moni sat at the far end to my right, turned away from me and talking to Shishir further to her right. Between her and us were Shishir's two friends. Shishir and she were talking, but not audibly. Her face was turned to him, and I could see that he was gesturing with two fingers slightly up above his head and seemed to be explaining something to her. I wondered what that was about.

Then Moni turned back to face the stage, where someone had begun to sing. Her fingers were fidgeting with her handbag and then a tissue came out of there. She glanced towards me and I was shocked to see there were tears shimmering in her eyes, but not flowing. Chichi had no idea, I think, because he was looking at the stage and the singer now. The singer was in the middle of a pretty competent rendition of '*Poochho na kaisay maine raiin bitayi*'.

But half a minute later, Moni had quietly pushed back her chair and was headed to the restroom. I got up too, and Dhruvi frowned slightly at me because the man who was singing noticed me getting up.

In the restroom, Moni was already dry-eyed and smiling thinly at the mirror. 'All of you said how nice I was looking, even his friends, and he hadn't said anything, so the idiot that I am I asked him "How am I looking in this sari, Shishir?" And you know what he said? He smiled and said, "I'm a graphics guy, babe, my visual benchmarks are a bit high, you know that . . ."'

Moni was making a grotesque effort not to cry by pushing her eyebrows up, right up, and grimacing so that her cheeks behaved like boulders against her eyes; and her jaw she set in a firm lock, almost grinding her teeth. I would have found it funny if I wasn't so incensed.

'Chutia Chichi,' I said, not caring who heard in the other restroom stalls. 'Is this pig for real?'

And this Moni, instead of being angry with the fellow, asks me, 'Tell me the truth, Viva, am I looking like . . . like the back of a bus? I know I can't wear saris too well . . .'

'I will not listen to this kind of stupid talk from you, do you hear me?' I said loudly, firmly.

Someone flushed a toilet, discreetly slid out of the door and left the restroom.

'You have got to let go of this swinish character, do you hear me, Moni?' I said fiercely, and this time it was my teeth almost grinding! 'His "visual benchmarks are too high" is that what he says?' I asked.

She just nodded numbly, but there was no time for more on the subject because we heard Shishir's name being called and it was his turn to sing.

Moni hurried out of the loo and back to her seat and I went back to mine. I was seething, and then I was appalled when it dawned on me what that gesture of his was earlier. With his two pudgy fingers twiddling horizontally above his big fat forehead, he must have been showing her how high his bloody 'visual benchmark' was.

He began his song – he had chosen to sing '*Laaga chunari mein daag*'. I was still mentally gagging on what Moni had told me, and couldn't pay much attention to the singing. But he seemed to be doing a half-decent job of it. When he was done, there was a good amount of applause and that idiot Moni clapped too. He came down off the stage and sat next to her. He leaned over towards us, and his friends said great, super and clapped him on his back.

He caught my eye and leaned further in, asking softly, 'How was I, Mrs Pradhan?'

I smiled at him, leant over, and said softly but distinctly, 'You were okay, Shishir, but umm . . .' and here I held my two fingers a little high in the air, just like he had before to Moni, and I said clearly, 'but you see, my auditory benchmarks are rather high, I'm afraid, so I'm not the right person to ask.'

One of his friends laughed nervously, Moni froze, Dhruv stared at me and Chichi's face shut down. His smug little expression turned in an instant into one of shock and then pure dislike. He turned pink, the lips turned downwards petulantly as if he might even blubber 'Mummy . . .' – which would have been fun to watch, but it didn't actually happen.

There was no question of dinner after that. I dropped Moni home in utter silence, except for small sniffs from her. She had got into the car without bothering with the sari now, and it sat slumped around her shoulders. Dhruvi sat very still at the back. She slipped out of the car and said a muffled goodnight to us, walking quickly into her gate, clutching the pleats of her sari in a fist and hitching it high as she hurried away. I saw the pretty dark-coffee sandals she wore and wanted to clobber that Chichi with those very sandals and then string them round his neck.

As we were going up the lift, Dhruv asked me why I had been so rude to Shishir. And I said the one thing that all young people hate to hear, 'you're too young to understand'. He looked reproachfully at me, so I rephrased that slightly to 'I'll tell you some other time, soon.'

At home, I switched on my computer. I found a question waiting to be answered for the agony aunt column that I sometimes helped a friend write. It was for a man's magazine, one of those snappy answers kind of columns, but gave sound advice. In one of those strange coincidences, this question seemed to have come from yet another cad. Must be some sort of epidemic of cadaria.

I'm 34, and been seeing this girl for the last few months. Problem is, I don't yet want to be 'seen' with her, as in she-me an item. I am running out of excuses and elaborate detours to not land up at parties with her or to not leave with her. I think she suspects something. She's fun and likes me a lot. I don't want to lose her. But I don't want the 'taken' chhaap on me yet. Still looking for greener pastures. Got any tips on how to manage this one?

I bashed out the answer hard on the keyboard, till Dhruvi called out from his bed in the other room: 'Viyaa, don't bang so hard on the keyboard, Viyaa, it will get spoilt.'

I wrote: *For starters, you could tell this girl that you're treating her to a facial and then bribe the cosmetologist to perform a lobotomy on her. Then she won't notice whatever jerk-like manoeuvres you come up with. If that involves spending more money than you're prepared to part with on this thing, just tell her you work night shifts and can only meet her for an hour or so at 7 am when your shift is over. Fix up to meet in places like underneath some half-built flyover. If anyone sees you there, just get out of your car and kick the tyres, open the boot and get her to look inside, so anybody who sees you with her thinks she's just your mechanic. This way, any of the phataka types that you don't want to lose out on will simply not catch on that you're seeing someone.*

Of course, chances are that she'll check with her buddies about all this and they'll first laugh themselves sick, tell her that she's up against a commitment-phobic, and then introduce her to a much better-looking and together man. And that will be that. But it's worth a try. And then you can head for those 'greener pastures', where you'll find the stupid cow that you deserve.

I hit the send button and lay down on Ashwin's side of the bed. Moni's held-back tears, shining like bits of glass in her soft black eyes, is what I saw when I shut my eyes.

5

Shruggy Shru

Besides saying it so I could swat that Chichi like a fly, the other night at that karaoke thing of his, I do actually have a 'high auditory benchmark'.

And my hearing is getting better and better as I age, can you believe it? I can hear far-off sounds clearly, better than most people. Maybe it is my work with dogs that is making me that way. Just by association.

Even through the sounds of Mumbai, I can hear the voice of the extremely earnest but touchingly talentless young girl four buildings away, soldiering on with her music lesson; my ears can also pick up the sound of her Masterji correcting her and trying to coax the right notes from her. I once mentioned it to Farhaan (my paper mosaic-artist neighbour on the third floor) and his partner and tried to get them to tune in, but they couldn't hear a thing. 'Mercifully,' as he said. He then warned me that if I was acquiring canine hearing capabilities, it wouldn't be long before I began to put my head up and emit a soft woeful howl whenever the girl began to sing, like some dogs do.

I had had a strictly exchange-of-interesting-leftovers relationship with Farhaan and his painter partner. Nothing more, nothing less. After Ashwin's passing, they had done me a small portrait of him in black and white paper pieces (in which his likeness to Guru Dutt was even more pronounced). We had since then added the occasional tea break, if we spotted each other on our balconies and one of them signalled with two enquiring index fingers: T?

It isn't just far-off sounds that I can catch. I hear all the microtones between two notes, I really do. I wouldn't be able to sing them or anything, but I can hear them for sure. And so we had named our daughter Shruti. A shruti is the smallest interval of pitch that the ear can detect between two notes – there is something so subtle and nuanced about a shruti. Our son Rishabh had been born when we were caught up with the insistent and obvious demands of a new marriage. Shruti came along a little later, when Ashwin and I were more finely tuned to each other, able to read between the high notes of each other's talk, to hear the microtones of each other's soul. And this is what we felt she was born out of, our daughter Shruti.

When did it begin then, the disharmony between me and this daughter of mine? She's thirty-four now, and it seems as if we've forever been in that place of dissonance that simply cannot correct itself. It was not that way through her growing years. She was a quiet but sweet child. Yet somewhere along the way, the quietness became a tendency to sulk and the sweetness had turned into a cool collectedness that I found unnerving.

Here's a good example: we were in Japan for a year because Ashwin was posted there. Shruti and Rishabh used to collect some little discs, I forget what they were called – tazos? pazos? something . . . They came with packets of chips and biscuits and all kinds of other packaged snacks. If you collected fifty by some date, you could exchange them for some action-hero figure or a watch. As the date for this came close, both my kids had only thirty-six of those tazos-pazos. They needed fourteen more and began to badger me to buy more stuff so that they got their fifty. I remember saying no, and trying to explain to them how beyond a point one must not be led by the nose by marketers into buying things you don't really need.

Shruti was eleven and Rishabh thirteen then, and I thought they had sort of understood my point. He was disappointed, but left it at that. She sulked and glowered at me for a few hours. In the evening, when she was packing her school bag, she told me in her new cool-collected voice, 'By Friday I will have fifty, you'll see.'

I didn't pay attention and thought it was an idle boast. But on Friday evening she came back from school, tossed fifty tazos-pazos on the dining table and said, 'Take me to the shop, Ma, I have to collect my gift.'

Here's what she had done, she told us. From a family album, she had taken out a picture of herself dressed in a Kashmiri outfit, from our vacation there when she was about seven years old. For two days in the lunch-recess, she had asked in the schoolyard, 'Who wants to see a picture of an Indian princess? Stand in line and give me one tazo to take a look.' Apparently a contingent of little Japanese and American classmates stood in a queue, handed her one tazo each, and got to peer at her photograph. And that's how she got her fourteen remaining tazos.

Ashwin and I took her to the shop, where she would get a pink wristwatch, she had already decided. On the way there, we were all quiet in the car. Rishabh, out of not having the required number of tazos, Shruti out of a quiet, focused excitement over the gift she was going to collect, and Ashwin and I out of shock and awe. We didn't quite know what to make of this – was it enterprising, or was it . . . we didn't quite know the word for it. Ashwin had laughed uncertainly that night and said, 'Well she didn't give up, and she got what she wanted. And she didn't cheat anyone . . .' But I remember we weren't exactly pleased.

But the real trouble between her and me began, officially, when Shruti decided that she wanted to go to the US straight after junior college, for under-grad studies, in 1994. People around us then weren't sending off their kids like that, the way they do today, breaking their bank or planning way in advance to amass a small fortune so that they can send off their Pappu or Tina to some random American university for an even more random set of subjects. Most of those that were going were going on scholarships, after graduating from here, or by taking student loans. Only a handful of Shruti's classmates were being sent off abroad, all expenses paid by parents. To Ashwin and me, they seemed more to be going on suitable boy-catching missions. The degree was just by the way. And they were from families that could afford this modern-day equivalent of a dowry.

When Shruti first mentioned it, it was the day after her seventeenth birthday, in 1994. She'd been writing off to foreign universities and brochures had been arriving in the post (this was just before the Internet changed all that). She had zeroed in on two universities. We thought she was making early plans for much later. But when she said at the breakfast table, 'Pa, by April next year the university will need Rs 4 lakh . . .,' Ashwin had looked incredulous, and had said, 'Let's talk this evening.' He had left for work, giving me a cautioning look.

I knew his look meant 'don't discuss it till I come back' and I should have kept quiet, but then that wouldn't have been me. I 'rounded on' her as Shruti would later describe it, and said, 'Where have you got the idea that we have this kind of money, Shruti?'

She didn't reply to that, and said, 'It's a liberal arts education, Ma, not some faltu timepass BA in History from here. And they'll let me study world history, comparative religions, population studies, the environment . . .'

'I'm not asking for the comparative merits of a degree from here and from there, Shru, I'm sure it's great, whatever it is they let you study there. I'm asking you how you came up with the idea that we can afford this for you. Most people look for scholarships, assistance, supporting work . . . no?'

'There aren't any scholarships or assistance at this level, they've made that very clear,' she said briskly, as if it was *me* applying to *her* for something.

I then descended into 'a lecture' about us being employed people and not business families that may be at liberty to send their daughters to get some obscure foreign degree, catch a perfect Indian engineer from their own community who would then return to the business-family fold, and all of that. I could see her freezing up and when I ended with 'do a degree from one of the better colleges here and try your luck with scholarships for higher studies in the US'; she muttered something again about faltu timepass degrees.

When I brought up the huge money outlay that she was expecting from us, Rs 4 lakh just for starters, I veered into territory that I should have left to her father to tackle: had she thought about what this would mean for our own future, buying a place to live after Ashwin's retirement, and all of that. I could hear my own voice in my head sounding so 'you' against 'us', but I couldn't quite stop, because instead of offering any sign to me that she had thought of any of this, she only regarded me coolly, and finally said, 'Let me hear what Dad has to say.' Again, I had that uncanny feeling that we were on test here, that we were appearing for an interview that was being conducted by Shruti.

That night, when Ashwin came home for work and said more or less what I had said, but in a nicer way than I had managed, all Shruti said in the end was to me, 'I see you've worked on him and both of you have decided that I'm fit only to waste three years pfaffing around some city college.'

'Your Ma has not "worked on me", Shruti,' Ashwin said loudly. And then in a kinder, more placatory tone, 'It's not the end of the world, Shru. People have done fantastic things with their lives after graduating from here. I know this liberal arts thing in the US looks extremely exciting, but you'll do it one day, on your own, Shru.'

From here on, she entered what her brother called the Shruggy-Shru phase. Most of her communication with us involved a range of shrugs, from the nonchalant to the eloquently sarcastic. She obtusely worked at getting just pass marks, and flatly refused to be drawn into any field trips and stuff that her rather-decent Mumbai college arranged.

Shruti did go to the US some years later, on her own steam, on a scholarship-fellowship. She pointedly applied for assistance even for her ticket to the US, though this was something Ashwin told her he would be happy to pay for. 'Don't need your donation,' she had said coolly.

She returned with a good degree, but now fuming about all things American. She then disappeared deep into the innards of rural India, and would emerge once in a while, ill and pissed off with yet another person that she had worked with in yet another developmental agency in yet another state.

Five years ago, inexplicably, appallingly, my angry little girl's kidneys packed up. This time, though, we did have something to offer her. A donation, but one that she simply had to take. She has Ashwin's kidney. 'Now not only do you have my staid-boring genes, you have my staid-boring kidney too, Shru,' he would tease.

And no, he didn't pass away because of kidney-related causes. It was his heart that let us down.

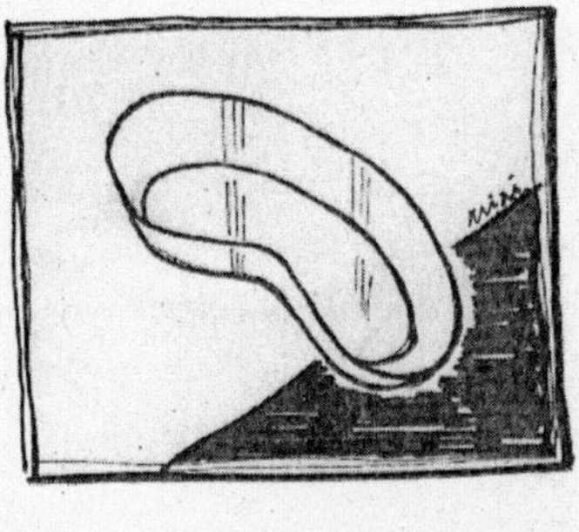

6

Dateless Diary

Shruti was doing okay, and working again with some people in rural Rajasthan who she had originally dismissed as 'non-serious' and 'stupid stooges'. She was now calmer, less out-of-joint, and even smiled gamely when her brother Rishabh asked her 'what news of the running dogs of capitalism?' and other such tired old jokes.

She had once asked me point-blank, soon after Ashwin passed away, 'Do you blame me for Dad's death?' It had all gotten too much and I had begun to weep and found that I could not stop. I wished even then that I could have answered her coolly, maturely, reassuringly, but I just cried on formlessly. And through my tears and weariness, I saw Shruti's petulance give way to a stricken expression. She was crouching near me and muttering, 'Sorry, Ma, I know it was his heart, not the kidney donation . . . but my shrink said I should . . .'

My tears evaporated suddenly, like someone had wrenched shut a tap, and I said, 'Your shrink is a copper-plated bastard if he's putting these thoughts in your head . . .' And Shruti had actually held my head to her stomach and gone 'Shh . . . shh . . . sorry, Mom, shh'. (Don't ask me the etymology of 'copper-plated bastard', but it was one of Ashwin and his batchmates' favourite gaalis for ruthless-manipulative people. One of his friends claimed that it came from a

James Hadley Chase novel, but I don't know for sure; it just felt like a fitting term for some people, and it rolled off the tongue well.)

Something had quite perceptibly shifted in Shruti after that visit. Now when she came to Mumbai, I noticed little changes in her. Even the way that she combed out her mass of curly shoulder-length hair was less angry now; the brush made soft, almost considerate-sounding strokes, rather than the customary brisk crackle of hair being punished into place. About six thread-white hairs showed at each temple, which I thought looked very pretty and almost artificial, like she had coloured them to look older for some school-play. But I didn't say this to her.

She had traded some of her shapeless clothes for better-fitted kurtas and slim-cut women's trousers (what we used to call slacks when we were young) and she looked really quite nice. But for at least eighteen of her thirty-four years, Shruti had received compliments of any sort with a Ninotchka-like glassy stare at the unsuspecting compliment-giver. So I didn't say anything about the nicer hair, the prettier clothes, her more relaxed and healthier appearance . . .

We could talk about her health, yes. And she would dutifully show me check-up reports, update me on her diet and exercise routines, even choose to share a strictly occasional glass of beer with me and drink nothing when she went out with friends. I counted that as an honour, and I'm not being sarcastic here. (Shruti knew the word sarcastic when she was very little – only she used to never remember how to say it right. 'No need to be sistercat with me,' she would glower at Ashwin when he was mildly sarcastic with the kids, and we would fall about laughing.)

Overall, Shruti and I were better now. Not great, but better.

The last time that she was here, I found myself actually telling her about a date (isn't there a more senior-citizen word for this, must we share the word with teenagers and twenty-somethings and feel foolish while using it?) that someone had set up for me. I hadn't told even my son Rishabh and Dharani, my daughter-in-law. I idly wondered about what Dhruvi would feel and think, if anything came of it, this date of mine. I had told Moni, and she had been in a state of controlled excitement and tension over it. She was neatly and painfully divided down the middle – she wanted me to meet someone nice, but she felt disloyal to Ashwin. I found myself calming her nerves first and then taking stock of mine.

One of Ashwin's friends had called up and asked me to go dine out with him and his wife, where they asked if I was at all willing to 'meet' someone.

'Do I have to?' I had first asked.

'Well there's no "have to", but we could all easily live for another 25 years, Viva . . .'

The words companion and looking for companionship were used repeatedly, nervously, in this conversation, which I took to mean 'not marriage necessarily'. And that sounded sort of okay to me. He was a senior bureaucrat, about to retire, had lost his wife a couple of years ago. I consulted myself and my Ashwin-self too – the part that was still a couple with Ashwin, well over two years after he had gone. Both selves said, go meet. Do go meet this Raghav Potential companion.

We exchanged emails at first, no photographs or anything. He wrote about his grown kids, his work, his wife's brief and brutal illness. It was nice, I can tell you, the emails. Playing blind-man's bluff, but with the assurance that there were no sharp surfaces around to cut you suddenly. Because both of us had been sort of vetted and pre-approved by our common friends as stable, non-psycho and innocent bystander victims of disease and death; not people with nasty twisted marriages behind us.

Till one day, about two weeks later, Raghav quickened the pace by sending me his phone number and asking for mine. By evening he had called me with a day, time and restaurant, and we were figuring out how to recognize each other. He said he would recognize me. I asked him how, and he said, 'Because I cheated and googled you and your picture appeared on www.louulyladisofindia.com.' It was silly-cheesy and he knew it, but I was amused, and ya, faintly flattered at the effort rather than the words. He had seen my picture on a site about caregivers of kidney-transplant patients, actually. That's the only place my picture appears on the Internet.

We met at that new off-Colaba Causeway place where the chef-owner combines strange and wondrous things. The two menu cards given to us were printed specially for 'Raghav and Guest'. There it was in print, Raghav and Guest on top of the menu. Kind of impressive, and I found myself wanting to tell Ashwin about this fancy new corporate-courtesy gesture.

I ordered the most intriguing sounding Fillet of Vietnamese Basa with Dalimbi Usal. It also sounded like it was not messy-slurpy-fussy to eat on a first meeting. Raghav ordered one more of 'whatever the lady is having'. I didn't see the point of two orders of the same thing, but it was plated food, and anyway we wouldn't be doing that comfy thing of going halfsies with two different dishes, like I would have with Ashwin, or Moni or any of my kids or friends. It was the same with the drinks; I ordered a cucumber daiquiri, and he said again to the waiter, 'Whatever the lady is having,' and he smiled at me. I realized he was being jokey-chivalrous, and decided it was nice. It was a bit of charm-phekoing, as we used to call it – which meant casually throwing charm at you, but it was okay.

Only after we had ordered did I realize that I hadn't quite looked at this man fully, and he too had busied himself with the wine list. He was already sitting at the table when I came in, and as he rose, I registered iron-grey hair and eyes that did a quick up-down-up glance at my 5ft 6 inches which I had clad in beige trousers and a burnt-orange jute blouse with a boat neck (my favourite kind of summer neck). I had worn flat slip-ons, and he must have been not a whole lot taller than me. In the old days, we would have called him 'dapper'. I don't know if anyone uses that word anymore. He was wearing a dove-grey-blue shirt and khakis. I liked what I saw.

Well, we had a nice time, talking about food, kids, grandchildren, departed spouses, childhoods, work. We slipped in some of our non-negotiables quite expertly, I would say. For instance, I managed to mention my reluctance for dressing up and playing hostess anymore, without sounding like I had hated doing it for Ashwin and without sounding like a budding bag-lady. Quite a feat. He managed to work in how his ancestral property in Juhu was already being divvied up between his grown kids (ergo: don't value me by that property, it's not in the reckoning). This was getting dangerously close to what are called 'pre-nup' arrangements, when there were going to be no nups. But I suppose these things had to be touched upon, however *en passant*, right at the outset.

We left when the Colaba by-lane got quiet, and the restaurant began winding up for the night. He lived in Worli at the time, and I lived further up at Shivaji Park. I insisted that he didn't have to come right up to my place, drop me and loop back to his home, and that I would make my way onwards. When he got off at his guest-house gate, Raghav looked uncertainly inside the cab, and said distinctly to me, so that the cab driver would register, 'Phone karo, please, once you have reached.'

'Don't worry about me,' I said airily.

(*Mistake No.1:* 'Letting a man, right on the first date, know that You Can Manage Well On Your Own,' Moni had later said – like I need advice from this Moni now on how to deal deftly with men.)

He emailed the same night, telling me he was going to be busy over the next few days, and that he forgot to tell me something exciting, that he was being flown to an offshore oil rig by helicopter – a first for him – as part of his winding-up duties before he retired fully. I liked the boyish enthusiasm about the helicopter ride, frankly, and the fact that he felt like telling me this little nugget of information. We were to meet the following week.

There were a couple more emails, but to cut a short story shorter, over the next few days, suddenly there seemed to be a reserve and a restraint from him. I had been my usual non-protocol-bound self, and written him several random emails telling him about some of my dog photography work of the next few days, asking him some more stuff about himself and throwing up the idea that the next time we could have dinner at my place.

These mails of mine were answered dutifully; the boyish charm had been turned off abruptly, firmly. No commitments were forthcoming about future meetings. I even wondered if some male-secretary was answering the mails for him. Absurd I know, but that's how mystifying it was, this change in tone. I went over the evening again, looked through some of my mails to him, and tried to think what I had done that could be defined as a deal-breaker, as they call it, and I could think of nothing. It didn't feel right, and I couldn't just drop it and let it go in my head.

How had I found myself in this utterly ridiculous spot where you jump off the trapeze and the person who has to reach out to hold you, simply folds his arms and watches? And all this in the senior-citizen's circus?

I called him once, and he sounded like somebody had died. He then called back late that night, and it went something like this, 'I liked this neighbour girl when we were both just teenagers. But at twenty-two, before I left for the US for higher studies, her parents insisted we become engaged. Actually I wanted to play the field a bit and not be committed to anyone just yet. But the girl was in an awkward position as the whole neighbourhood and her family expected us to marry, and remember this was the early 1970s. So I married her the next year, and remained faithful to her and she was a good wife and mother. But last week, a day or two after I met you, a woman junior to me from college days turned up in my life; she is separated from her husband now, and says she was crazy about me in college and still holds a torch for me. I really do want to now "check out my market" if you pardon the expression, albeit late in life. I've been a good husband till my wife's last days, now I do want to soar and cruise a bit if possible. I hope you understand.'

'Ouch', as Moni said when I told her. And 'bugger', as Shruti put it.

Here's how you make Fillet of Vietnamese Basa with Dalimbi Usal like they served at that tony restaurant (serves two):

> The usal

Buy or make 2 cups of sprouted dalimbi/vaal (field beans); use fava beans if you don't get these; but dalimbis/vaal have that sharp taste that goes well with the mild fish.

Heat oil in a kadhai, add mustard seeds and let them splutter; add a pinch of hing, haldi, 6 curry leaves and the dalimbi;

Stir and cover the kadhai for 2-3 minutes.

Add a glass of hot water and cook till the beans become soft.

Throw in jaggery/sugar, salt, red chilli powder according to taste

Now throw in a teaspoon of ground jeera and a tablespoon of dry grated coconut, and cook for 2-3 minutes.

Introduce half a cup of ground fresh coconut and simmer for a minute.

Add chopped green coriander and a few steamed cashew nuts.

> The fish

(I read a news report that said 'the rapid spread and acceptance in India of the Vietnamese Basa in the past three years has left experts baffled and beaming'. So get some if you can, but any firm white fish that your fish-wallah will fillet for you is as good.)

Rub one lemon and a little salt and half a teaspoon of minced garlic on 2 fillets. Grill lightly in a pan or under a grille with a little olive or sesame oil. Transfer on to a plate.

Heap a bit of dalimbi usal on the side, letting some of its juices slide under the fish. Garnish with really thin slanted slivers of fresh red and green chillies (or not, if you are fussy or wussy about chillies).

7

Fang and Claw

For me, it was quite a *huh?* moment, that Raghav man's 180-degree turn. I hadn't seen it coming. How could I have? I would have thought that stepping out to go on a date at sixty-plus would not have been fraught with such sudden twists and turns. I had felt that it had gone quite well, our some weeks of emails and one long evening out together. And since I had made myself cross over to the idea of being with someone else after Ashwin, now I felt even more . . . what is the word . . . 'cheated'? No, too big a word for too small an episode. Clearly, this was not about him and me, it was about him and him, and I sort of understood what the man felt he wanted to do when he said he wanted to 'check out his market' even if it was late in life. And all the best to him, I thought.

About six weeks later though, there was email from Raghav, without a subject line – often a sign that the emailer and the content of the email is so distressed that the person just could not sum it up in the subject line. And so it was. The sum and substance of his mail: the woman he had met – the one that had 'held a torch for him through all her years of a bad marriage with a philandering adman' – had actually been trying to get her husband to feel jealous and to look at her with new eyes. It had worked wonders and she was back in her marriage with a duly chastised husband (who must have hurriedly crumpled up and thrown away some of the extra women in *his* life, I am thinking). The added distress for Raghav was that just about everyone else in their circle knew what she had been playing at except himself. 'Perhaps what I need is a dose of your no-nonsense company, Viva' is what he ended the mail with.

Well, I thought, you wanted to 'soar and cruise', as you put it, at sixty-two; then you must also be prepared to get sore and bruise. Honestly, I didn't want to jeer or gloat, even in my mind, at this stranger who had veered briefly on to my path, but I certainly didn't want to be his agony aunt or 'relationship coach' as they call it, now that he had taken a pratfall. Nor did I want to explore going out with him again, if that is what he expected. It had felt cold, alone and stupid, the few days when I thought we had something going and he had withdrawn. I didn't have it in me, I realized fully, to go through the feints and ploys of this kind of 'dating'.

So I respectfully deleted his email without replying. Respectfully meaning I didn't gloat, or use my middle finger to delete it, or mutter eff-off while doing it. I just deleted it.

I did tell Farhaan about it, by email, and not by visiting him downstairs, because I knew he was in the thick of one of his paper mosaics. I wrote to him about the Vietnamese Basa fish dish too. All that he sent back as a reply was this little nugget of info:

'Basa fish are farmed along the Mekong River – one of the most polluted rivers in the world. Heavy industries along this river frequently dump extremely toxic waste directly into it. The US Food and Drug Administration imposed increased and more thorough testing on Southeast Asian farm-raised seafood, including *the basa* (that was Farhaan's emphasis) after repeatedly discovering fish contaminated with heavy metals and banned antibiotics.'

But the next week, when he invited me down to his studio for tea, he said without looking up from his meticulous pincer-and-paper mosaic work, 'At least you know now that you are ready to mingle.'

'Hardly,' I said. And at that he looked over his glasses, directly at me, a longish stare. Farhaan was not big on eye contact, normally.

'Look, look, keep looking at me,' I said. 'It's good for your eyes to focus away from your work. And while you're at it, look out of the window too. You got to change focus at least every fifteen minutes for your eyes to last you.' His partner, Orup, gave me an encouraging nod over his shoulder. It was one of those couple moments that a third person steps into, where you say something that endorses what one part of the couple has been nagging the other about. Though nagging was a strong word for these two almost soundless, usually monosyllabic creatures.

I parted the curtain slowly, carefully, so that Farhaan would look out of his window. You couldn't move anything suddenly around him and cause air to move, because he had little trays full of cut or torn paper bits for his mosaics on his table. In Farhaan's craft, every 'stroke of the brush' was actually a piece of cut paper.

He was in the middle of a three-feet-long and two-feet-high mural. It was dense grass and foliage in very many shades of green; there was only a hint of burnt-orange and black and barely there white interwoven in all this green. It was part of his Ranthambore triptych (that later got picked up by someone for an 'obscene' sum of money, which we celebrated in their customary quiet but extremely bizarre way, but more on that later).

Farhaan had recently moved away from his equally wonderful geometrics – my favourite was a row of arched Mughal-style stables, all in shades of beige, basalt, sandstone, and red agra stone, with just one deep blue horse waiting in one of the arches. Some of his works made you feel as if he had visited your dreams and borrowed his images from there.

Orup worked at another intricate skill – he was doing a book on Indian trees, painting them like portraits of people: picking up the demeanour and attitude of each tree perfectly, its fallen flowers lying exactly, exactly like you see them. His backgrounds were abstract and in perfect sync with the realism of the tree paintings itself. After seeing his work, trees that I've always loved have become more beautiful and their particular ways of holding or dropping their leaves and flowers have become more attractive to me when I pass them. The accompanying text in this book is to be little extracts about that tree from Indian classical poetry and botanical information on the tree, on the opposite page. Each page-spread is to have Orup's painting, the extract and the information.

The lady who is doing the text, to Orup's utter horror, is loud, voluble, but a well-respected botanist and extremely good at her work, so he can't even whine to his publisher to get someone else, he says. Left to Orup, he would do his paintings and then go into hiding, only to emerge when the book was out in print. But the talkative tree-expert will hear nothing of it and calls him up every time she comes upon a fitting quote from old texts.

Which must be perfectly natural for her. And I venture to say to him that some of the references that she reads out must surely inspire and inform his paintings?

'Jangly' is all he says by way of reply.

One day she appeared at the studio uninvited, because he wouldn't pick up his phone. She had extracts from a classical poem called *Soundarananda*, in which there are references to the kadamb tree, which he had finished painting in all its magnificence. She simply had to share with him the poet's description of its spreading branches under which Shiva and Parvati and/or Radha and Krishna spent many amorous hours. The botanist, also once a dancer, read out the extract with many flashing eye expressions and mudras, with Orup watching her warily. Farhaan had left the room a little earlier, after carefully placing paperweights on all of his work, seeing that the lady was dancing up a mini-storm.

The lady ended with a snatch from an old song '*Kadamb ki*

Chhaya'. I applauded far too loudly, to make up for the stony silence with which her exuberance was received. She picked up her bag and said the tree's botanical name out loud fondly, *Neolamarckia cadamba*, as if talking about a favourite child, then skipped away, quite unaware of how much she had rattled Orup.

There is about both Farhaan and Orup almost an aversion to words and language. I am careful, when I visit for tea, to stay well within my quota of how much I should talk. Telling Farhaan about my date-that-wasn't, even if by email, I must have used up plenty of my talk-time with them already.

I left their studio and stepped out with my camera. I had fallen behind in my work slightly. This dog project was something that Moni had sent my way. Aidan Skene, a Scottish vet and now researcher, was in India to document the Indian dog – from the Mudhol Hounds and Rajapalyams to the pariahs, street dogs, mongrels and a range of distinct nomenclatures that I was yet to master. His mails referred to the Indian Native Dog, INDog, in which he was very interested, and to also the mixing in of European breeds with our local dogs over the centuries. My only qualification was that I had time and that I did not fear the street dogs of Mumbai.

We hadn't had a dog in the house for a while now; at first because Ashwin's job kept us in big-city downtown apartments, and then since Shruti's kidney issue, there were hygiene fears. But I grew up with a jumble of mixed mutts in the house. Photography wasn't particularly my thing either, but the man wanted photographs for documentation and not as high art, and the camera that he sent me was smart.

An additional qualification (which I had not told Aidan Skene for fear of appearing like I was overselling myself for a simple job, and also for fear of him thinking of me as some unscientific dog-koochy-koo type) was that, for long now, random dogs tended to walk up to me and look me straight in the eye. And I could clearly see on their faces questions, complaints, requests; some did that adho-mukha shvanasan thing of prostrating themselves first, then sitting in the HMV dog pose or the Sphinx pose and looking searchingly at me. I often found myself asking them, 'What?'

It had become a bit of a running joke between Ashwin and me, especially when we used to speak about our plans for retiring into the hills. 'Bag Lady with Entourage will be you walking into the local market with three or four canines following at a respectful distance.'

I never fed them or petted them, any of the dogs, wherever I lived, but 'You notice them, and look at them with a sort of "and who are you and where are you going" way,' Ashwin once pointed out. A few months before his passing, we had vacationed in Ranikhet up in the hills of north India, and there, believe it or not, one ash-grey dog took to leaving a piece of dry chapatti right on the single step of our cottage every morning.

Ashwin had advanced his theories to greater heights then. 'See, they have begun to leave you little offerings in the mornings, prashad. Soon they will build you a mandir – Shvaneshvari Mata Mandir.'

But I didn't tell Aidan Skene any of this, of course. Hardly the right thing to tell a vet and cynologist (a new word for me). I hadn't met this vet from Scotland yet; we had only spoken on the phone and he had mailed me with his requirements. A big voice he had, and I imagined he looked like the large pink Father Tonner of my childhood, who walked cheerfully and purposefully house-to-house every evening, visiting his parish in the Mumbai suburb that I grew up in.

After a stint in Mainpur, Aidan was currently camped in Mudhol in Karnataka, and was going to come into Maharashtra when his work with the Mudhol Hound story was done. It was an everyday variety of digital camera that Aidan had sent to me, and I had to take pictures of as many colours, sizes, shapes, ear and tail variations as I could and email them to him every few days.

It felt good to get into work and drop any of the residual ridiculousness that I had felt over the date that wasn't.

Today I set out to photograph some of the black-and-white short-coated street dogs. As I crouched and aimed at the mosaic-patterned creature sitting outside the istriwallah's, she furled her lip slightly and growled . . . it sounded sort of like 'paparazzi'.

I stepped back quickly and said, 'What??'

She looked away sheepishly and the growl petered out into 'err . . . nothing'.

8

Sandwiches and Shandy

I woke up to a racing heartbeat, drumming-thrumming in my head and chest. Which is either the cause or the effect, I can never tell which, of a recurring dream in the last year or so. The dream was always something to do with having to wind up and pack up from a hotel or guest house to catch a train. In the dream, I am overwhelmed by the way I have spread out my things, rooted down in this temporary place, though I should have known better. I have acquired too much stuff, my suitcases are not large enough, and I have to simply leave with whatever fits in one of them. I cram in a few things after agonizing about what to take and what to leave behind.

Always, in this dream, I race towards the train on foot, with just the one suitcase in hand. I then realize with a shock that the train will stop at a signal and not at the platform, and there is no one around who will give me a hand. Now the single suitcase will have to be left by the wayside too; I feel wrenched and unwilling to part with it. I consider sitting on the side and letting the train pass. But that is not an option in the dream, and I must leave the bag and prepare to clamber up the train steps using both my hands during its brief halt.

I am walking now on the ankle-twisting small stones laid on the side of the rail track. As the train stops, I reach up to clutch at the iron-rung steps. This is the point at which I wake up, my heart thudding at something like 120 per minute. I lie quietly in bed, breathing steadily, purposefully, so that I hear my pulse slow down and quieten in my ears.

It is an intimation-of-mortality dream, I'm pretty sure. The signals are clear: one day you will have to exit, so start winding up your pasara, as the philosophers call it – the paraphernalia of living. And even when you do wind it up, you'll still be hanging on to at least one suitcase full of things-people-notions that you simply can't bear to be without. But they will have to be left too, because the train will have come for you, and you have to get on minus any of those things. And clambering on will not be easy either; you will have to do it alone, unaided.

But I don't tell this dream, and its variations that recur, to anyone. The one time I mentioned it to my son Rishabh and his wife Dharani, they instantly said I must go get my cardio status checked. They were not in the least interested in the hidden meaning of the dream, but only in the fact that my heart was racing, right in my sleep, even when I was not exercising or active. Moni and my daughter and the downstairs chaps might be intrigued by the imagery of the dream, but they too would prick up their ears and point hospital-wards, so I kept it to myself. I intend getting to the end of my days without tangling with any doctors as far as possible. So best to keep quiet.

I met a soulmate in this matter once, on the train from Pune back to Mumbai. I was wearing snug socks, because it gets cold in the compartment. The lady next to me – I must have been fifty-two or so and she must have been what I am now, sixty or a little more – a small round woman, cheerfully asked me the usual questions about husband, children, caste, etc as soon as the train started. Then, eyeing my socks, she said regretfully that she should have got a pair for herself. And so casually, with not a hint of pity-garnering or alarm-mongering, she told me that she had been quite ill the previous night.

The description sounded like she had definitely had what would appear as 'significant changes in her ECG' at the very least! Sweating, left side tingling, mild hanger-shaped neck and shoulder pains, jaw pains. She could have woken up her neighbours, but she knew she would be driven speedily to a hospital and that would interfere with her upcoming fun-plans. So she simply lay very, very still, she said, and 'took the name of Shirdi Saibaba and Jhulelal'. The night passed. In the morning she got dressed, packed a few clothes and requested a neighbour to drop her to the station.

She was now on her way to Mumbai to meet her daughter and son-in-law and a five-year-old grandchild, who were flying in from 'Ceylon', as she called it, staying at the President, shopping for two full days and flying off. They had invited her to join them on their Mumbai spree. A cardiac episode was the kind of annoying interruption that no one needed, she had decided. She had promised her gods that, upon her return to Pune, she would get a full check-up. In the mean time, one of her gods had told her in one of her dreams: *keep your feet warm.* But she had forgotten to pack socks and not realized how cold the air-conditioned compartment could get.

Instead of exhorting her to go see a doctor as soon as she reached Mumbai and get her priorities right and all that jazz, I offered her my socks; I had worn them for barely half an hour, if she wouldn't mind. She said yes immediately, and once they were on, even a passing doubt that she may have had about her health was gone and she nattered on happily. When it was time to alight, she asked me if I would like my socks delivered back to me washed and ironed, by courier, and I said, no ma'am. Never met her again, but I remember her well.

Today, I have the suitcase-train dream during an afternoon nap. Once my heart stops thudding and I feel okay again, I get up and get dressed. Aidan Skene has arrived in Mumbai to meet his fellow cynologists in the INdog project. We plan to meet, but not in a restaurant; he asks if I would mind walking along Marine Drive early evening. I assume he still does not have the stomach for Indian and/or restaurant food.

We have one of those cell-phone moments when two strangers are talking to each other on the phone, not realizing that they are just twenty feet from each other, and finally I spot him and wave. He drops his phone into his pocket and walks towards me. Aidan is not at all like the hefty, ruddy Scottish Father Tonner of my childhood that his name and big voice had conjured up.

He has been in India for a while now, and this is not his first trip. I knew that. But I had not expected someone so . . . so merged-looking. He has totally melded with the Marine Drive walkers at the place where we are to meet, and I have passed him twice, I realize later.

Aidan is wiry, compact; early to mid-fifties, I am guessing. He is wearing a white cotton half-sleeved shirt and baggy grey trousers. He has a gent's leather belt in his hand that he seems to have just bought from a man walking away with a bunch of them on his arm. He has white close-cut hair and a near-Indian skin tone. It is not a tan – it seems to be his colour. The eyes are not Indian; they are classic comic-book blue, as if coloured with a turquoise sketch pen, set deep into his face. The nose is flattish, sunburnt slightly. The overall effect is quite Indian. Not just the colour, but something about him.

We get past the immediate awkwardness of a first meeting as he hands me his new belt to hold, with a 'could you please . . .' while he quickly takes off the canvas one that he had on, walks to a bin and throws it away. He takes the new one from me and wears it, clicking the buckle in place with a satisfied smile. All right there on Marine Drive.

'Should we walk towards Nariman Point or towards Chowpatty?' he asks.

I take a couple of seconds to respond because it is taking me a few beats for the phone-voice Aidan and this man in front of me to form a composite.

He seems to read my thoughts, and says, as we fall into stride towards Chowpatty, 'Please tell me you didn't expect a Scotsman in a kilt playing the bagpipes, with one black and one white terrier gambolling at his feet?'

'No, but something like a big blonde Jesuit priest dabbing sweat from his pink forehead and wearing a white cassock and beaming benignly,' I say.

'Sorry to disappoint . . . lass,' he says. The 'lass' was added as a sly afterthought – his attempt at playing the cliché of a Scotsman in my head.

His maternal grandfather had been from India, found and adopted as a baby by a missionary couple in the late 1800s, somewhere in Bijapur state in the south. They returned first to England and then to Scotland, where the adopted Indian boy grew up, married a Scottish woman, Aidan informed me. 'So I could well have been wearing a cassock if he had continued with his parents' stock-in-trade, you know,' he concluded.

His big voice – it wasn't loud so much as big, like it came from a much larger body – was a good thing, because the evening traffic had begun on Marine Drive, and my right ear was doing its disconcerting block-unblock thing.

We sat on the sea wall as the sun coloured the water orange and the sky peach. In the middle of planning the next few days of work, Aidan pulled out his wallet, took out someone's visiting card and smiling to himself, passed it on to me.

'I can never really keep up with the way India moves, however much I pretend,' he said. 'But you tell me, would you too not wonder at this? Can you guess what this man does for a living? A chap in the share-taxi gave it to me.'

The card said 'Mohit Mehta, Alien Co-ordinator'. There was a north Mumbai number and address. For a micro-second there, I wondered if I had come upon one of those big gaps in information that you experience. You know the kind, where everyone around knows about some development and you have not a clue. Somehow, in spite of the newspapers and the shouting news channels, you have just not heard of something. Was this one of those things – were there aliens visiting so regularly that they needed earthly co-ordinators like this Mohit Mehta? It was just a passing flash of outlandish theory in my head, I knew, but I couldn't come to any obvious explanation either. Suddenly I felt unreasonably irrelevant and out of sync with everything around me, but the moment passed.

Aidan put a hand under my elbow and said, 'The colour's all gone from your face, Viva, you okay there?'

'Do tell, what this Alien Co-ordinator does,' I said, but the words came out faint and faraway, I could hear myself.

'I think we should get you something to eat or drink maybe?' he asked.

I thought I should; because the slight wooziness could not be out of just feeling disorientated by the fact that I had never heard of a profession like Alien Co-ordinator. We crossed over to Café Ideal.

Once I had eaten half of a large soft-grilled chicken sandwich, I did feel much better. Aidan was drinking beer, and I had him top up my lemonade with some of it. Shandy.

'Okay, give up?' Aidan asked. 'Shall I tell you what an Alien Co-ordinator does?'

9

Castles in the Air

The mystifying job description, Alien Co-ordinator, was simply a man who worked in Bollywood, and arranged for 'foreigners' to appear in the background or in cameo appearances in a Hindi film. Earlier, you could just take on a few wide-eyed tourists to fill these parts. Now, the Co-ordinator who Aidan had met in a share-taxi explained, the film industry is required to get itself more organized. And this is where the Alien Co-ordinator came in. 'Gora-log or kala-log or cheeni-log or arabi-log' – and these were the aliens – could be found for the small parts, but now their papers had to be looked at carefully, police clearance taken, a temporary work permit made for them and only then could they be hired under the 'junior artist' category. And it wasn't just gosh-golly tourists, who came on for a lark, that you could rope in now. Small-time actors from other countries hankered to get on a Bolly set, even if it meant that they were part of a crowd scene. The Alien Co-ordinator got paid by the film producer as well as by any 'firangi' that he could 'fit' in an Indian film.

To Aidan's extreme amusement, the man had slid him his card and informed him that he could fit him in, and in more than just a background scene. Even though he was not 'ekdum gora', he had 'prsnalty', the Alien Co-ordinator had added. I could just see Aidan as a night-club owner in the older Hindi pictures, or in a new Bolly film as some kindly yacht owner on the Riviera who lets Katrina and Akshay, or some such, hide in his boat while the bad guys look for them.

They were called 'extras' when I was young, today's 'junior artists'. In those movies, they stood around in a party scene in which Dharmendra sang while pretend-plinking at a grand piano and the heroine looked demure or devastated, depending on the situation. Or the extras made up the 'murmur' crowd in a courtroom scene. When something shocking was revealed in court, this lot of junior artists, playing the seated spectators, was instructed to turn to one another and say in low voices 'murmur-murmur-murmur', so that their lips moved and a low drone could be heard. The judge could then do the thing with his gavel and call out sternly, 'Arder, aarder!' Aidan tells me that they were called the 'walla-walla' crowd in old Hollywood films. They went 'walla-walla-walla' when a muted uproar was to be produced in a scene.

We step out of Ideal Café. Aidan's solicitousness is over, now that I am fed and steady on my feet again. He walks briskly, and I will soon learn that these walking-meetings are an Aidan speciality. Before we part, he tells me the bizarre and unsubstantiated story that he has unearthed in his research. It is about a nawab who decided to go to Pakistan after the partitioning of India. A known animal lover (and credited with saving the Asiatic Lion from extinction by his conservation efforts), he is said to have, last-minute, taken his dogs and left behind his wives when he fled in a plane (this is the completely unconfirmed part of the story).

Aidan has only recently come upon the story and finds it immensely interesting, the choices that people faced during India's Independence. This particular nawab decided to secede his princely state to Pakistan, though it was surrounded by what would be Indian territory. Finding his choice really most inconvenient, the Indian government moved in on him with the help of some of his own people. This is when the nawab decided to exit on a plane, taking only his twelve canines, as the story goes. True or not, Aidan finds this enduring factoid enormously funny and endearing, and is laughing helplessly even as he is telling it to me standing on the pavement.

We fix our next appointment for three days later, for which Aidan will unfortunately have to sit down in one place, in my house, at the computer. I wonder to myself if he is capable of it or whether I will have to shout firmly, Sit! Stay! His spry and spare frame now disappears into the sodium-vapour light as he crosses the road and walks up towards Walkeshwar, his temporary home at a fellow cynologist's apartment. I sink into a cab and head home.

The next day is going to be one I have been hoping to dodge for some weeks now. But there's no escaping it. I have yet another meeting with the lawyer. Each and every meeting (five so far) has ended with me feeling dull-witted, sad and vengeful – a kaleidoscope of emotions that end up cancelling out the others, till I block them all out. Until the next time that I have to get this matter moving.

It's like this: Ashwin left me a surprise that has turned sour. It is the kind of thing that, had he been alive, we would have had many disagreements about. A strange miscalculation on his part about what I would like, what would work for us, who he should trust. All done in good faith, I have no doubt, but really most unsuitable. And doubly so, now that he is gone.

Almost two years ago, on my sixtieth birthday, I was away in Pune to spend the day with Dhruvi. It was about five months after Ashwin had passed away, and one of his colleagues, Bipin, called up to wish me. This was a family that we had spent some good times with; our kids had been friends when Ashwin and he were posted at the same place, off and on; we had taken a few vacations together. There were two other couples like this.

What Ashwin had done, while he and I were still talking about buying land in the hills somewhere, was to quietly put down money in a joint venture with these three colleagues. A big plot of land that would get divided four ways. He planned to present it to me on my sixtieth is what the person who called me said. The paperwork was done, and the colleagues thought they should give me my copy on my birthday and invite me to drive up with them to see it.

A small tremor of something like irritation passed through me then, as if Ashwin was still there and I could go take issue with him on this decision. It died down shamefacedly, that odd moment, and I heard Bipin going on, 'It was a damn decent price, and we also figured that we'll get a good deal whenever we decide to build our houses too, if we all work together with one contractor.'

There was no point, me wondering what the heck Ashwin had been thinking when he just went ahead and bought this place. Of course he had been thinking that it was a good deal, it was with like-minded people, and that buying out there somewhere all alone would not have been a good idea for us. Of course he wanted to give me a pleasant surprise. And of course, now that he had gone, even if he had not planned it that way, I was in safe company, with people I knew, if I still wanted to go live in the hills. But I felt robbed of the pleasure of the search, the discussion, the drives to and fro, consulting Rishabh, Dharani, Dhruv, Shruti, Moni. Here I was with a site-unseen gift, and not at all certain that I wanted these people as the neighbours of my twilight years. And I felt like an utter heel for feeling all of this.

This was over two years ago. I had pulled myself together a few days later, and gone with Bipin and his wife and a couple of the others with whom I was now firmly tied round the neck in this scheme to see the place. It was pretty, no doubt, on a hill on the backwaters of a dam, a five-hour drive from Mumbai, closer from Pune. And when I thought of Ashwin pulling it all together to surprise me, I wanted to weep at my loss and also at my inability to feel fully grateful for this parting gift.

Over the ensuing months, there were many even less savoury things that began to emerge from this surprise package. And each time that I encountered one of them, I would think silently, guiltily, 'Ashwin, what have you gone and done.'

To start with, none of the other three parties had any intention of beginning to build there, not for at least another seven or eight years, easily. One of them only thought of it as a great investment and a 'bit of Indian soil to leave to the grandkids', he said. Secondly, when I tried to meet them all, to talk about what my options were with the place, I found it hard to get them to commit a date when we could all meet. A couple of the women in this group were in that Poor Viva mode, and when we met at the club, I was served understanding nods, tea and biscuits plunked down by surly waiters and a helping of prettily evasive answers.

I left feeling as if I had behaved like 'such a junglee' as they would say – because I tried at least four times to cut through the blather about Munni at Harvard and Toto at Stanford and Pinky's gap year in Brazil and what not, and persisted with my questions, 'So how do we take this forward, I want to meet the guys too, I need to know if I can put my own fence and start to build a structure, you know, I'm going to use a local boy to build for me, a simple three rooms and a veranda, I want to put down trees in some places.' They would only smile and look away politely, as if someone had broken wind noisily or something.

And this is how it's been. I've got no answers from anyone, except soothing 'Viva, your land and your investment is *completely* safe, don't *worry*, darling' from a couple of the men. When it dawned on me that months had gone by, and I was less and less likely to begin with this dream-home thing of mine, I met a lawyer that my son recommended. He first suggested that the others buy me out. When I went back with that suggestion, it only fetched me a couple of more teas and soothing phone calls. I went quiet for a while, doing the ostrich thing, but when I did haul myself to the lawyer again, he said, 'Well none of them are really *obliged* to buy you out. There's no document made about the internal arrangements between the four families. And the agreement between the landowner and you chaps, that's rather shaky too, frankly. And I'm surprised . . . really, why didn't any of you involve a lawyer when doing this deal?'

Ya, why, Ashwin?

Tomorrow is my sixth visit to this lawyer. He had last suggested that I find someone to buy my share, so that I just get out of this thing. I had asked around, and no one had exactly snapped up the offer. But one of my son's friends had shown interest some weeks ago, and even gone and taken a look at the place. However, the Triumvirate had, after many emails up and down, indicated that they didn't want to have an unknown person in on the arrangement.

One of them, Bipin or Neeraj, I forget which, ended with a 'Hang in there, Viva, we want *only you* as a neighbour, sweetie. If it's about the money, and you need a bridge loan, you *just* have to say the word.'

The insincere, patronizing pig.

10

Armed and Dangerous

The lawyer, I can see, is rapidly losing interest in my 'case' if I can even call it that. All his earlier talk of 'fast-track option because you are senior citizen, Pradhan Madam' is replaced with 'out-of-court settlement is best option'. When I tell him that none of the other plot-owners is interested in settling anything, I see that he is looking switched off and bored.

To get me to get up and go home, he says as kindly as he can, 'Mrs Pradhan, Madam, the original paperwork for that plot is weak – the saat/bara is not in any of you people's name, co-owners are not taking this as an urgent matter. Do them a favour and tell them that they should at least do that paperwork or no one will get anything. Original owner's three sisters and four brothers will sprout from the ground and say he sold it without their consent. Then? *Then*?'

I said nothing. As if I would know what then? then? I wanted to redirect those Thens to Ashwin, but I instantly told myself to shut up. I needed to stop letting this thing become a tiff between Ashwin and me. Little black dots tumbled downwards at the periphery of my vision. Always a sign that the merry-go-round of exasperation, sadness and helplessness was going to start up in my head. Ashwin would be sitting out of reach on one of the tinny metal horses of this merry-go-round, I on another, the lawyer on another, our so-called friends, co-owners of that plot, would be on other rusty multicoloured horses; and now the merry-go-round was getting crowded with potential new claimants to the plot that the lawyer had just warned me about. And the whole thing would begin to whirl and whirl and whirl, without any of us ever catching up with each other or co-operating in any way. A lurching centrifuge of intentions, dreams, plans, schemes, hopes, fears, lies, let downs, betrayals, promises and paperwork.

The lawyer was asking me something – and I wasn't sure I had heard him right. 'Madam, have you ever been cheated of money, had a robbery in your house, had your bag snatched with plenty of money in it, lost jewellery?'

'No, none of the above,' I replied, wondering where we were headed with this.

'Then, see, you count as if sum-total of such things which have not happened to you, have happened now, in this land deal. Aapka pocket cut ho gaya aisa samjho.'

Well I don't need you to help me rationalize this situation, I wanted to tell him, but I let it go. In his own way, he was trying to be helpful though mine was a dud case for him, clearly. He began to fiddle around with the things on his table and called out to someone to get two chais. He scribbled a number on his writing pad, tore the piece of paper smartly off like he had written me a prescription and passed it to me. 'You call him. He may be able to make your friends see some sense. Also may take care of original owner.'

He had written the words '*Gautam-Gafoor*' and a cell number.

I realized I was being shunted. Like those doctors who have a patient whose case is in some twilight zone that defies diagnosis or treatment – they begin to send him and his relatives hither and thither, wheeling him off to specialists, path labs, MRI centres and to any new hospital machinery that needs to be tried out. The unsaid words are: 'anywhere but here'. The lawyer too seemed to have decided that it was time to shunt me off to Erewhon and beyond.

I got off his visitor's chair and I could almost hear the relief.

'Who is this? Is this one person or two people?' I asked, waving the folded prescription paper at him, as I exited his door, demonstrating clearly to him that yes I was leaving.

'Oh, Gautam-Gafoor. He is almost a lawyer. Good for such matters,' he said.

What is 'almost a lawyer', I didn't bother to ask. I pushed the paper into my handbag and left.

At home, I did the sequence of static exercises that I had promised my grandson I would not skip, even if I missed doing them in the morning. One of them involved a shrug – not many shrugs, just one sustained shrug held for a minute with two-kg weights in both hands. For this, I had doggedly refused to buy the pretty pink 'ladies weights' or let Moni or my son get them for me. I had two Bisleri plastic bottles filled with sand, which I used instead. I could grip them at their waist, and go into the shrug.

My wardrobe and accessories culling was coming along well, and I just did not want to replace old paraphernalia of living with new ageing-lady stuff, especially stuff to exercise with. That's also why I refused to have three different reading glasses all over the place, and had been resisting my son's offer of a Kindle and an iPad and all of that. He laughed at my heavy old laptop that could not be taken anywhere and routinely offered me upgrades, but always backed off when I said a firm 'no, Rishabh'.

Only my daughter Shruti had looked at my home-grown cottage-industry dumbbells and given something like a small smile of approval. She and the kids and women that she worked with in Rajasthan were currently making a compound wall out of old mineral water bottles filled with local sand, laid on their side and piled up row upon row. She used only the common computer on which the kids were learning at their centre, and did not own a cell phone. Given her health background, I wished she would have one, but we had three numbers for her where she always got messages or could be called to the phone, and she called dutifully every few weeks.

It is Saturday and Moni arrives. Today I am giving her a selection from my kitchen stuff – crockery, glasses, bakeware, brass handis from my grandmother's home, salad bowls from Ashwin and my travels, and all of that. She is going to help me divide it up, wrap it and put it into boxes marked Dharani and Moni.

Moni takes out the large punch bowl with the gorgeous grape pattern in pale green crystal at its lip, and without checking with me, puts it firmly in Rishabh–Dharani's box. She knows its origins. It was Ashwin's gift on my fiftieth birthday. And it wasn't something he just gave me. It was something that I came upon at the end of a most elaborately set up day that he had packed with little surprises for me. I know Moni will ask me, like a kid, to tell her about that day again. She knows it already, the whole fiftieth birthday thing that Ashwin co-ordinated. But she likes to hear the story. And perhaps it is time to revisit that gossamer day, what with my recent mental mutterings about Ashwin's plot-of-land gift that is turning out to be such a pain.

We have tea and tiny mini-rusks. I watch Moni float a few into her hot tea, like croutons; she then quickly spoons them out and slurps them up before they get too soggy. Her dark eyes shine like a child's as she concentrates on this activity. I wonder briefly if her Shishir Chichi with his 'high visual benchmark' would approve of such things.

We spoke about him only once, since his karaoke evening where he made her cry. I can only think of that evening in these simple terms: *that* Shishir made *my* Moni cry. But the one time that we did speak about it a few days later, Moni seemed to have bought into his explanation wholesale. Chichi insisted that she had been oversensitive, that it was *she* who had asked *him* how she looked, and he was only responding as a graphic artist, telling her how the visual world presented itself to him. And so his remark about 'having high visual benchmarks' was about himself and not about her, and that perhaps she was carrying some sort of baggage and that's why she was being hypersensitive.

I could see that the swine Shishir was what psychologists called 'gaslighting' Moni. It's that thing where a self-absorbed cruel person manages to make the other person always doubt her own perceptions of an incident and convince her that her emotions are all wrong and out of line. I watched Moni explaining away her hurt and anger of the karaoke evening to me, and I did not snort and throw some choice cusswords around. There seemed to be no point. When I did not react at all, Moni clammed up.

Neither of us refer to Shishir Chichi after that. I hope that I will hear of him only when she has deleted him from her life. Meanwhile, Moni has probably decided that she will talk about him only when there is something good and substantial to tell me. But until either of these scenarios actually come true, I know she must be still seeing him, tiptoeing around him and settling for crumbs from his table, waiting and praying and telling herself that he 'needs time', as if dealing with some skittish and refined breed of horse that needed to be broken in gently.

The doorbell rings, and Moni returns to tell me that there are two policemen at the door. I have that fearful and pointlessly guilty twinge in my stomach that policemen always evoke. But they are only going house to house in our area, visiting senior citizens who live alone. Moni smartly asks them for their IDs and examines them carefully, even taking down their names and badge numbers. They are slightly surprised, but one of them looks at her approvingly and says, 'Good, alert citizenry is a very good thing, Ma'am.' He provides all the details, including the current chowki in-charge, phone numbers and all of that.

They are polite, well-spoken young men, and they do their job well. They have been trained to caution people without frightening them. As I watch and listen to them, a silly lump rises in my throat – it is some mixture of pride and gratitude and feeling good about India and its youth and stuff like that, in the midst of the general decay and disheartening stuff that's on the telly all the time. I'm surprised at my sentimentality, and swallow firmly before replying to their questions about door locks, balcony grills, etc. They suggest I keep a loud metal whistle at hand at night and never ever go to investigate any odd sounds in the balcony or at the door or windows myself. Only blow the whistle loudly and insistently, right from your bed, they advise. Moni looks like she may giggle, but she composes her face quickly. They recommend that I shut my bedroom door at night and lock it from inside, isolating myself from the rest of the apartment for the night.

I don't tell them about it, but when they are gone, I show Moni the fake-pistol under my pillow that I have been keeping since the spate of burglaries of the last some months. It is a rather good Diwali pistol. It has a snub nose and a dull, menacing metallic finish. Only the effect is somewhat spoiled by the letters *SHERIF* embossed on one side, and *COURT MARSHAALL* on the other. Moni laughs so hard that she says she has to go pee. She comes back and hugs me tight.

'You are armed and dangerous now, Viva.'

Before she leaves with her package of crockery, I tell her briefly about my pointless visit to the lawyer, and about the oddly named Gautam-Gafoor, 'the almost a lawyer' whose number I have been given.

'Must be a minor thug with a law degree from the University of Internetcity or something,' she concludes. 'Call me if you do decide to go see him.'

11

Finding Pressed Flowers

The full-grown white dog who used to follow his mother around in my lane has been transformed suddenly into a sober sort. I have photographed him and his mother – a low-slung white creature I've seen for the last twelve years. Spunky, really her own person, this dog. The goofy son was one of the last of many of her litters over the years. He is a bit thick and kind of never left the nest. He has hung around her even when fully grown. He has none of the charm and chutzpah of his mother. Bow legged, rat-tailed, gawky, the duffer would usually be hanging vacantly around her, while she busily got food, staved off trespassing dogs and did ten other bustly things that she must have done all of her street life.

Some days back, I saw him not looking so goofy anymore. And I knew at once, from his entire demeanour, that his mom had gone – she must have easily been thirteen or fourteen years old, the old girl. The Goof is now suddenly too aggressive, watching his back, running about randomly, guarding the lane ferociously, looking what could have been comical, but I didn't feel like smiling. The Goof is, I think, experiencing the thing that happens when a parent or loved partner goes. Suddenly, a layer is gone between you and the hard sunlight, between you and the darkening sky, between you and the wolf at the door. You have to do it all yourself now, and no amount of hanging around that efficient parent/spouse of yours has prepared you to hack it on your own.

I must have looked a lot like Goof soon after Ashwin passed away – especially when I entered the bank, or when I sat blank-minded across the table at the accountant's, when I listened dully to the safety-door guy obviously ramping up his charges because I was an 'akela senior ladies' as he put it. And like Goof, I too either caved without a whimper, or took needlessly belligerent stances at all of this.

And here I was again, probably headed to making a silly goof of myself with this plot-of-land thing. That it had turned out to be Ashwin's posthumous gift made it difficult for me to simply walk away and cut my losses, which is something that my son had obliquely suggested. I was attached to the notion of this plot. And yet the feeling that Ashwin seemed to have left me with a bit of a hot potato as a sixtieth birthday gift just won't go away. So I did what I knew best in the matter – just pushed it out of my head, till it snaked up in my mind again.

Aidan was coming over to work on our dog documentation, and had shouted down the phone, 'D'you and Moni eat prawns? Then just make some rice, I'm getting the rest.' His big booming voice I figured was also used to more effect in India, allowing him to hear himself above the roar of traffic and the screech of marble-cutting machinery that was the anthem of this city. Before I could ask him why, and should he be cooking fish at his veggie-sounding host's place, he had hung up.

He is at the door at noon with a bright green plastic shopping basket, looking quite the Mumbaikar, except for the turquoise eyes and matching linen scarf slung around his neck, with paw-prints woven into it. From the basket, he carefully pulls out three tender coconuts, whose sliced tops have been re-sealed with wheat-dough, like you do the lid of a biryani pot.

We sit down to eat, and he offers to serve. He places a coconut on each side plate. He heaps some warm rice on our plates and then taps open the dried dough seal of the coconut. From the inside, he scoops and spoons out the contents on to our rice. It is about five-to-six medium-sized prawns wrapped in a sort of velvet 'curry' of thin white tender coconut, red chilli scraps and some other flavourings. It looks pretty, white on white, on a hot day. It tastes sensational, and Aidan takes several bows at our exclamations. And no, his one Indian grandparent has nothing to do with this recipe, he tells Moni, as she watches him with a sort of awed curiosity. He tells us it is something that he has learnt and synthesized from his stays in West Bengal and Karnataka.

Aidan's tender coconut prawns

Prepare one coconut per person.

Buy tender coconut with the cap lopped off, but retain the cap.

Drink up the water, leaving just about a tablespoon in there. Leave the soft coconut, the 'malai', intact.

Go home and put in 6-8 cleaned prawns in the coconut cavity with salt and a couple of slivers of ginger.

Make a tadka tempering of karipatta, one slit green chilli, one red chilli in scraps and mustard seeds, and add that.

Shut each coconut with its own cap, and flatten some wheat dough around the slit so that it is thoroughly sealed.

Put it into a pre-heated oven and bake at 180°C for about 20 min, and till the dough seal looks dry.

Scrape away the dried seal, open the coconut cap, and scraping the tender coconut from the sides, mix and mash slightly. Now scrape out all of it with the prawns on to a small mound of warm rice.

White wine or beer is a good idea.

It is Moni's forty-second birthday, and for reasons that I don't go into, she is not spending any part of it with Chichi. She's going out later with what I think of as her 'normal' friends – people who don't make her cry. Before Aidan and I get down to work after lunch, Moni wheedles my fiftieth-birthday story from me. For me, and now for her, that story is like coming upon pressed flowers in an old book.

It goes something like this: a week or so before my fiftieth birthday, Ashwin had asked me what I wanted to do on that day. I am not in a great mood, in the midst of one of those sullen phases with Shruti. She was about twenty-one then, and staying at home before she got the scholarship for the US. She would not allow the maid to clean her room (she did not believe in 'slavery', as she put it). And yet she would not simply clean it herself. It had become, I felt, a health hazard and was beyond a joke.

Even our most casual conversations were a wearying chess game that usually went something like this:

(Shruti at the breakfast table, Ashwin getting ready for work, me at the kitchen counter.)

'So what are you doing today, Shru, more applications?'

'Nothing.'

When I turn around, I get the feeling that she has stopped doing something abruptly, something that I don't like – like pulling out mustard seeds from her plate of poha and arranging them on the edge of her plate.

'Your grandma's been asking to see you.'

Blank stare.

'Maybe you could visit tomorrow.'

She advances a defensive pawn, *'I have work tomorrow.'*

'Let's watch a film together tonight.'

'I'm going out.' Check!

'With friends.' Check!

'I'll be late.' Check!

'Don't wait up for me.' Check!

'Shru, your room . . . can we . . .'

'Nothing wrong with my room.' Checkmate!

On one such day, after she left, I stepped into her room. It seemed to be holding the fort for her. It held her surly secrets. The furniture watched me, dead-pan; the bed seemed to be lounging insouciantly, insolent; the chairs were frozen in their sitting positions, watchful; the desk surface expectant, lying in wait. The posters held their breath as I looked at them. There was Che and Fidel and some other charlies and a couple of angry-looking women on the wall.

I lay on the floor and shut my eyes, the stiff silence telling me that I shouldn't be there. Just like when Shruti wanted me out of the room. The curtains billowed and fell back sharply, impatient, bordering on the rude. I got up and put on her computer. It came on obediently, but not readily. I began a game of chess with it. It played like Shruti – focused, sure-footed, unafraid of spilling blood. My every move was answered too quickly, too challengingly. Queens taken, bishops defrocked, horses put down, elephants hunted. Check! and Check! and Check! Only a few pawns and my king wandered about listlessly. I switched off the computer. It smirked shut.

I then took my duster and began to wipe the top of the desk. I rubbed it till it squealed. 'You got a problem?' I asked. Shocked silence. I shook out the rug and bed cover, plumped the pillows, shook the curtains, pulled stuff out from under the bed, straightened the books, files, racquets, shoes and flicked a duster over the posters. I almost heard gasps. Then I cleaned every crevice of the keyboard, dusted the screen, covered it.

'Checkmate!' I shouted over my shoulder and left the room.

You can imagine that none of this had gone down well with Shruti. 'Invasion of privacy', 'bourgeois obsession with order' and other such phrases were flung about, to Ashwin's amusement and my shame-anger.

This was the mood at home, and also 9/11 had just happened. So when Ashwin asked me what I wanted to do for my approaching fiftieth birthday, I said, 'I want to just walk somewhere nice, on my own for a bit. Maybe I'll walk up Malabar Hill and on to Naaz Café at the top.' (Naaz existed then.)

He had said okay, and could he join me for chai and bun-maska up there later? Which seemed like a nice enough plan. I planned to take a bus to the base of Walkeshwar from where we lived in south Mumbai, then walk up to Teen Batti, take a sharp turn right and on to the top of Malabar Hill to Naaz.

At the Cuffe Parade bus stop, I bumped into an old school teacher of mine that we had all adored and I had stayed in touch with off and on – Zia Karim, who taught us history, often with tears in her eyes, and events of the past were never the same boring thing for us ever again. I didn't tell her it was my birthday, but when we found seats on the bus, she urged a beautiful metal-leaf filigree bookmark on me that she took out from her book, saying, 'Keep this, Vibhavari.' We got off at Walkeshwar and she went her way.

As I began my upward walk, with the sea roaring and assaulting the rocks to my left at high tide, someone waved to me from the opposite side of the road. I wasn't sure who it was, then saw it was the doctor, the ob-gyn, who had a year previously delivered Dhruvi, or saved Dhruvi, depending on how one looks at it. This man's face had imprinted itself on my non-religious mind like a devotee holds on to the image of his god, I realized. I found myself doing almost a sajdaa, a sort of genuflecting; he crosses the road and asks after Dhruvi, walks a bit of the way with me and then crosses back to his side and down the other way.

And so it was, all along my walk up, people began to seem to randomly pop up from here and there, as if just by chance. That was how Ashwin had set it all up. People precious to me from my past, present and my future too, with Dhruvi, just a year old, and his parents, and Shruti (and the nice boy that she was seeing at the time) waiting up at the top for breakfast together. There were also two college friends and a couple of friends of the last some years, my brother and his wife from Indonesia, my only surviving relatives .... the mad fool Ashwin had arranged for them to show up along my route, each one going some of the distance with me. He had bought me the big crystal punch bowl for that birthday. And we had all gone home and made much punch.

Moni sighed and said, 'I wish I had been there . . .'

To which Aidan added, 'If you're going to wish, then wish big, Moni: wish that you have someone so into you when you hit fifty that he comes up with and pulls off a wild surprise like this one.'

Moni and I exchanged glances, and I kept a straight face. Somehow I could not see Chichi doing anything of the sort, and I suspect Moni too is not deluded enough to dream of it either. Aidan added: 'It doesn't have to be a spouse or lover, though . . . it can be a friend, a sister, a mother, anyone who will take all that trouble for you, and yes you must have enough true friends who will show up for such a caper . . .'

I see they are both, like anyone who has heard it before, quite taken up and enchanted by the story.

Whether Moni has cleverly drawn me back to the time that I basked so easily in Ashwin's grace and brio and good planning, I don't know. But that whole revisit to my fiftieth birthday helped me decide firmly that I would not question and fret over his last birthday gift that was turning into such a millstone. And instead of cringing from the whole process and taking random stabs at sorting it out, I would give it one very good shot – trying to get that plot clearly in my own name and maybe even building on it.

I pulled out Gautam-Gafoor's number. Now not only Moni, but Aidan too wanted to go along. 'I'll only be a fly on the wall, won't I?' Aidan pleaded. 'I've met many almosts in India – almost-a-doctor, almost-an-actor, almost-a-vet, almost-a-saint, almost-a-policeman . . . now I can come see what almost-a-lawyers do.'

I don't say yes or no. I'm not so sure I want an almost-white man in the equation when I go to this chap's place.

I dial the number, and the call is taken by a woman or maybe a child.

When I ask for him, the woman/child at the other end says sweetly, 'Spikking.'

I ask for Gautam-Gafoor again, and again a soft voice lisps, a little impatiently, 'Spikking, spikking.'

Luckily, I stop myself from saying, 'Papa ko bulao, call your papa.'

The man with the double-barrel name, I realize, has the voice of a sparrow.

12

Gautam-Gafoor Speaking

The last time that I had met Dhruvi, he did something to my phone. Instead of an ordinary ring when I got a call, it was his voice, saying 'Vivaaa, *pick up* the phone . . . Vivaaa, *pick up* the phone . . . Vivaaa, *pick up* the phone' in a rising crescendo way. He had done it without telling me, and if his intention was to make me wonder if I was losing my mind, he'd done a good job.

The first time that it rang, after Dhruvi had left for Pune, I froze at what seemed to be his voice coming from my bag. I was in the midst of telling a young woman and a man at the new supermarket how lousy their products were and why I loved my local shop dearly. I was waving a packet of sticky-smelly peas at them that had come out of their frozen foods section, and just as I was hitting the high notes and they were looking mildly interested, this new thing happened. Dhruvi's voice asking me to *pick up* the phone from inside my handbag.

I did think for a few seconds that the arrangement of my mind had got altered. Deranged, I believe the word would be. At first I thought the voice was on the PA system of the supermarket, and I could simply not figure how and why. Several explanations vroomed through my mind – maybe an FM radio programme on which Dhruv had called in and was calling me? Or he was hiding in one of the aisles of the supermarket, but how did he get there? Or I was hearing voices, but it was really too early for that – although I did have a family history of gone-colourfully-senile ancestors, so it could be . . .

When Dhruvi's voice kept going insistently louder, I realized it was coming from somewhere in my vicinity, in fact right from inside my handbag, and it was urging me to *pick up* my phone. My utter disorientation evaporated rapidly, and I took the call and managed to talk to whoever it was that had called me. By this time, the supermarket pair had quietly melted away, and I stood there with my packet of smelly-sticky peas, still determined to raise a stink about it.

I had earlier had small run-ins with the top-floor people who attended the clothing aisles in this place. It was there that I first realized that anyone over perhaps 40 is magically invisible to them. And me, at sixty-plus? I swear I could have danced, chanted, sat in a corner and read for eight hours, or fainted in one of the vertical-coffin changing rooms, and no one would have noticed. I had tried to get them to show me some clothes, but most of the young salespeople were deeply engrossed in fraught phone conversations whispered into their cell phones. One of them even ducked and pretended to tidy up a lower shelf when I approached her counter. From below there, I heard snatches of her conversation, in which she was asking someone archly-tartly, *'Mai aisa kabbbhi karegi kya? Tereko bharosa nahich hai na merepey?'* When I heard sniffing and a noisy blowing of a weepy nose, I knew that the chances of me being served were very slim. Life's more pressing demands on this girl were panning out in front of me, and I could take my silly request for tall-size 'jeggings' elsewhere. I shouldn't be buying clothing with newly coined names was perhaps the lesson here.

When I called Dhruvi and asked him what he had done with my phone and how I could change it back to a normal ring-tone, he hooted delightedly and said, 'Won't tell you, Viyaa.' I could have got Moni to fix it, or struggled my way through figuring it out, but I had just left it that way, and now I liked this ring-tone with his voice urging me to *pick-up* the phone. It did get me some odd looks in public places, but that was fine. I managed to lower the volume on it, so that it didn't appear to people that I had a kid trapped in my handbag.

Shruti, when she first heard this ring-tone, had burst out laughing, surprising everyone around her, like that princess in the fairytale for whom people were called from far and wide to try to make her smile. Shru had come for her check-up, which had gone fine, and she seemed more relaxed overall. She mentioned plans to travel to Nepal, and I assumed that it was on work. She was also learning to speak the language (she is absolutely brilliant with languages, and picks them up like other women her age pick up footwear). The night before she left to return to Rajasthan, she politely asked me if she could make an ISD call to Nepal, and I heard her speaking softly in Hindi laced with some Nepali phrases. I had not heard Shruti sounding so tender for a long while, and of course I wondered if it was a man. A man who spoke no English, only Hindi and Nepali?

She, of course, didn't volunteer any info after her call, and I didn't ask. I had thought I would tell her about my coming visit to Gautam-Gafoor, but she looked quite in her own world, and not in a surly way. So I thought I wouldn't burden her with the vexed arithmetic of my land deal. And her advice too, like my son's, would probably be to simply walk away from the whole thing.

The address at which I was to find the man was in a lane full of trading company shops and offices. It was an old congested part of town that was confusing rather than threatening, and I was happy that Moni had come with me. I had okayed Aidan's coming along too. His presence would be a bit unusual, but his almost-foreign almost-Indian looks would make him not stick out a lot. He came wearing very dark glasses, as part of some gangster joke in his head, and those hid his startling turquoise eyes.

The front part of Gautam-Gafoor's establishment was a soaps and detergents shop. A young boy asked us to sit on a small bench kept against the wall and returned with water. Moni and I sat, while Aidan began to wander in the little space, examining the goods. Massive packs of soaps and detergents sat around neatly, with brand names like Bhagya-Naseeb, Jyoti-Shama, Noor-Prakash. Moni leaned over to me and whispered, 'This guy takes the double-barrel Hindu–Muslim amity thing very seriously.'

We were then ushered in through a glass door at the back, and entered an office at which sat our man. He was well built, filling up his swivel chair fully. He must have been in his late thirties. There was a kind of massive, bulky gravitas to him. He looked like a rural Maharashtra policeman. His air conditioner must have been set at 12°C. (Later, Aidan told me that he was going to say 'Nobody asked us to pack for winter', but he kept very still and quiet, remaining in fly-on-the-wall mode as he had promised, with none of that Western-world ice-breaking banter that Moni had cautioned him against. I had promised him that I would ask in the end about the interesting name, if the meeting went well.)

Gautam-Gafoor's small dark eyes took in the three of us and invited us to sit. He signalled through his glass pane for tea, and put out his left hand for my papers. It felt good to see his thick hand engulfing my sad little sheaf of papers.

Though I had spoken to him on the phone, none of us were prepared for the sweet chirrup of a voice that emerged from this man.

'Other parties will not buy you out? This is not big money for you people.' There was no suggestion of mockery in the 'you people'. He just meant 'us types' – professional, urban, corporate backgrounds.

I could feel Moni and Aidan react to the voice. They sat up and stared like two kids, before quickly recovering.

He noticed them, and asked me in Hindi, 'Who are these of yours?'

I replied, for some reason, 'My niece and my late husband's cousin.' Silly of me, but somehow that sounded like I hadn't just brought along spectators.

To his buy-out question, part of me wanted to say sharply, 'If the other parties would buy me out, would I be here?' But I just nodded no.

He riffled through the papers again and twittered, 'Original owner also has just sold, without NOC from his relatives. He can't sell like this. All *gadbad* papers.'

He caught from the expression on my face that I knew all of this and quickly went on to enumerate, now in Marathi, what my options with him were: that he could send someone around to my plot-partners to 'see sense', he could also send someone around to the local land records office to make the man there 'see sense'. The third option, he almost took an advance bow in his chair before saying it, just one word that he delivered: *media*.

Apparently, he had 'reach' in the media, and how would I like the idea of being portrayed as wronged senior citizen, that too a widowed woman? Now he chirruped on rapidly, about how it would get everyone to sit up and listen. Whenever he used the word 'media', his hands formed a kind of camera-on-shoulder action.

He ended in English again, 'And then build your house and show your fancy plot-partners thenga.' He stuck out his thumb at the word thenga.

I looked straight at him and said in Marathi, severely, 'What media, what thenga, Gautambhai-Gafoorbhai?'

He shrugged and said in Gujarati now (we were clearly playing language musical chairs), 'Okay, sister, forget media for the time-being. We can start with just one of my boys going and explaining the problem to your friends, those co-owners. We will definitely get a mandowli from them.' A mandowli was gangsta- and tradesman-speak for a non-verbal, non-written agreement forced on someone.

'And why would they even meet your boys?' I asked sharply.

'That you leave to me,' he trilled. But his eyes and face were not being cute. He looked dead serious. It's just that his voice sounded so sweet, and there was nothing that he could do about that.

'See, your maamla is not big enough for us, really. What we can get from this? So I am suggesting, because you are a senior citizen, free for you, one visit to your co-owners from my two boys. After that, if you get positive result only, you can give something to them.' He indicated his pantheon of gods, pirs, babas, devis, matajis, saints and mother Marys on the wall behind him.

He signalled again through the glass panel for chai, and it came in tiny silver cups.

'You think about it, what you want to do,' he said.

I had visions of Ashwin's refined friends being visited by one of GG's boys, maybe at the Club! And about how that conversation would go. Would there be muted threats of physical violence? If they did actually meet one of the boys, either they would seriously soil their pants, or they would call up some senior police officer about this intimidation . . . and then I would be in real trouble.

GG looked at me and smiled for the first time. Beautiful graded square white teeth. 'Don't think so much, Pradhan madam,' he warbled. 'Just give your problem to us for now.'

His smile reminded me that I had promised Aidan I would ask about his name.

'I don't know who-all, who-all brought me up, different people, I was called Bablu,' he replied. 'Then my guru gave me this name when I passed. I was fifteen when he gave me my new name and my own piece,' he said, 'and this shop to manage.' (I knew from Hindi movies that they used the word 'ghoda' for a gun, but GG said 'piece', like in Hollywood.) He randomly added in Marathi, 'I can stop a Hindu–Muslim riot before it begins in this whole area and two adjoining areas.' I believed him.

'Gautam means wise and Gafoor means merciful,' he said, as he got himself out of his chair with surprising lightness and walked us to the door. 'Don't worry, I will be wise and merciful with your high-class co-owners, Mrs Pradhan. Only you have to think and you have to tell me what you want me to do,' he said in that dulcet voice. On the way out, he picked up a packet of detergent and handed it to Aidan, saying just the word 'Try' to him.

We marched in a single file down the gali and got into a taxi. No one spoke. Neither Moni nor Aidan made fun of that voice. Gautam-Gafoor and his soap shop had given us things to think about. Only when we were sitting at Kyani eating mutton sandwiches and drinking ice cream soda, did Aidan ask me, 'So what will you do, Viva?'

As was my habit with this frustrating land deal, my mind had now wandered very far away, and I was thinking of Shruti and her Nepal connection.

13

Shadow of the Falcon

Aidan was telling us something about a hotel in Abu Dhabi. '. . . So there's the pigeons shitting up its beautiful façade, right?'

I wondered idly apropos of what he was telling us this story. While my mind had wandered off after Shruti and her Nepal link, I had missed some parts of the conversation. I only came back to the here-and-now when I heard Moni saying severely but smiling, 'Viva *stop* making straw-pulling noises – your ice-cream soda is *over*, the bottle is *empty*. We can order you another one, but *please* stop that bottle-burp sound.'

'So this hotel façade, you know, the balconies, balustrades, eaves, cornices, *everything*, used to get coated in pigeon guano; wall-to-wall doo-doo. And their little down feathers would float down on to hotel guests and into the swimming pool. And sometimes chicks would fall down, splat. And the smell and the sight of the sun hitting all that shit . . . oh boy . . .'

'We get the idea,' Moni said, and pointed to the food around us as indication that a detailed description of faeces of any species was not called for, and particularly in Aidan's address-the-nation voice.

'So the owners, two brothers who kept a sort of personal zoo,' (Aidan was the vet at this place for a year) 'they hired this falconer, see?' he went on. 'In the off season. So that there wouldn't be tourists having to watch the massacre and mayhem that they expected. Four times a day, the falcon was let off and she would go right out into the sky, soar, then curve around and head straight for the pigeons. Just the sight of this *thing* coming at them would have them flying off in droves. Can you believe it, not a single pigeon was actually killed. The falconer would treat her to a chunk of meat when she returned to his sleeve. She knew that.'

I imagined this majestically named falcon, Mehjabeen, let out a shrill cry as she soared in the Abu Dhabi sky, then circled, wheeled and returned in a languid loop. Her shadow must be following her out, and then racing her back to the morsel of meat in the falconer's hand.

Was Aidan telling us this story, I wondered vaguely, to suggest that I hire a falconer (I met one once in Kutch) for the window-ledge pigeon pestilence that I periodically moaned about?

He rapped a fork smartly on the side of my plate, to get my attention, 'So my point is this, Viva: maybe just a visit from one of Gautam-Gafoor's boys may work like the shadow of a falcon with your fancy friends. It may scare them shitless too.'

I liked the idea, and this was clearly what GG had in mind. But a little red flag had come up in my mind right when GG was giving me his options. What if of one of these people called up some very big cop about being intimidated? The trail would lead straight to me and I would be in real trouble. They would have me for finger food at the next many parties, 'Poor Viva, she's really gone junglee, did you hear? She hired some two-bit goons to solve her issues . . .'

'It would probably get them to come up with some offer to sort your plot gochi, Viva,' Moni added.

'Gochi . . .' Aidan repeated almost to himself. He would, no doubt, use it effectively and appropriately somewhere.

When I told them my fears about this course of action, they fell silent. We stared at the small squares of mutton sandwiches in front of us as if at a chessboard.

Then Moni pronounced, 'It all depends on who has more "vatt", as they call it in these circles – who has more influence. You'll have to ask GG this doubt of yours, "what happens if my ex-buddies call in the big guns?" and from his answer you'll know how well-entrenched he is.'

'If he's all . . .' in a sweet tremolo she imitated GG, '"Arrey, Pradhan-madam, why you worry?" then you know he's got vatt. If he hems and haws and asks you to let him think about it, then you know he's unsure of his standing.'

Knowing that if I now went home without closing this thing, I would let it all drift again, I dialled GG's number and asked him my question. I came right out with it without any preamble: what if someone pulled some senior police contact and both he (and then I) got into trouble for intimidating people?

He replied with a small sigh, 'Are any of your co-owners political fellows, or contributing to political parties and all?'

I said, 'Not that I know of, most probably no.' After all, we have known each other over the years, and I think they are just the garden variety of successful corporate professionals. It is just unfortunate that their plans and mine for that plot of land are now completely at variance with each other.

'Then don't worry, Pradhan-madam,' he said. 'Just give me an indication, and I will put someone on it,' he said. 'FOC,' he added sweetly. I said I would call him in two days.

What the heck is Eff Oh See?

'Free of Cost,' Aidan supplied.

'And how do you know this?' I asked.

'Pradhan-madam, I am a Scotsman. I know every word or acronym there is to know which indicates a bargain or a freebie.' And so saying he picked up the bill and paid for it, ignoring our protests, and leapt down the two tall stone steps of Kyani, sort of swinging from the stout rope hanging there instead of a railing. We had planned to see a film in Metro across from the restaurant, but we were in the thick of our very own script right now.

'But why is Gautam-Gafoor offering to do this free?' Moni asked.

'It's small work, and it's a way to keep his falcons exercised . . . and he took a shine to Pradhan-madam,' Aidan said as he crossed the road smartly, while Moni and me shrank from the traffic.

When I reached home, I lay on Ashwin's side of the bed. I put on something randomly on my laptop from the 2,000 hours of concert recordings that he had got from a collector on an external hard disk. The disk was like a sleek slab of black chocolate, and on it Ashwin had hours and hours of old Hindi songs, Knopfler and Clapton, and Ella, and the Begum, and Mehdi Hasan and Hindustani Classical, with voices and instrumentalists from India and Pakistan, and people we had never heard of before. I loved to simply click anywhere and listen to what poured forth. Ashwin had not heard everything from this treasure-chest, and I have not yet listened to it all either.

I have a set of great headphones that my son has given me, and sometimes it is wonderful to block out all sounds and be inside the sound bubble. But on some days I like the music to come down like a drizzle and lightly coat all the objects in my room. I plugged in the speakers. It was a Kaushi Kannada on the sitar. Debu Chaudhuri. The melody, what is called the *pakad*, always made me think of someone asking questions of his god or of existence. They are not angry demanding questions, it is more of a seeking. Towards the end there is a gently sustained epiphany, a calm resolution. I had heard this recording before, and as the perfectly tuned instrument begins to sing in the hands of the player, I feel the events of the whole day slipping away from me. The notes slide alongside my body and I nestle against them.

I see Moni's number flashing on my mobile and I decide not to take it. I don't want to talk about 'the problem of Viva's plot' anymore, even if she is likely to be just checking in on me to see if

I'm okay. And if it is about some new piece of pomposity/meanness from her Chichi, I will not interrupt this celestial music for it. This is not a fair guess on my part, because Moni has determinedly stopped telling me about him right from the time of the karaoke evening. 'Tomorrow,' I message her firmly.

She barely holds her horses, it looks like, through the night. She is at my door at 8 a.m., and is looking flushed. A weight seems to have lifted off her, yet she is looking her forty-two years and not the young thing that she usually looks. She has had some kind of epiphany herself.

Moni has had the best antidote to a toxic substance like Shishir Chichi. She has, over the last few days, met first one and then another, two women who have also gone out with him before. They have spent last evening and late into the night filling each other in on the details and variations of his blithe bastardliness.

I almost feel a small pang of pity for the man. When the people who someone has mistreated get together and achieve critical mass (in this case two ex and one current girlfriends) there is going to be blood in the streets. And his head is going to be passed around like a rolling trophy.

Moni was pacing up and down my sitting room, and her entire demeanour was like a dog who has hunted a rat for the first time, and has now laid it out triumphantly on his owner's doormat. She was repeating herself, enjoying every phrase, and I was happy for her in a sort of grim-satisfaction way.

The only time her voice wavered and tears appeared briefly was when she said, 'And this I didn't tell you, Viva, but last week, one of the things he said was how my family was pretty dysfunctional – while his family, immediate and extended, had nary a divorce, no addictions, no gay/lesbian-coming-out, bankruptcy or drop-outs. And when I objected to his listing such things, he said, "Arrey, but backgrounds do count, no? Why are you being defensive? I'm just saying that I come from very stable stock, which is unusual nowadays, and not unimportant'

I wanted to sock him in his smug face. 'Not unimportant' – the rodent *would* use pompous double-negatives and be completely unaware of what hurt he was causing with his declarations. But this time Moni had enough outrage for the two of us. She was smirking now, a cool, dangerous looking smirk; all the humiliations, big and small, of the last year and more, which she had chosen to overlook, were now powering that smirk.

I felt that I should caution her to keep it short and specific when she told him off, and not to sound overwrought and over-the-top. He could easily turn superior and lofty on her. But she was having way too much fun with this, and perhaps Chi-Chi needed to hear some of it.

'I'm meeting him today. When I'm done with him, he will look like an empty, pichkaoed, punched-in Bisleri bottle. Of course he won't stay that way; the hot air inside him will fill out the dents and he will puff up again, but I won't be around to see that,' she said.

'And when you're done, you could offer your slaughter-services to Gautam-Gafoor,' I said, and tried to hug her. But Moni was in no hugging mood. She was all falcon, contemplating her quarry.

14

Motion Pictures in the Mind

For the last three seasons, I have not bought mangoes. Ashwin was the enthusiast, and did that old-world thing of sending off a crate each to his near and dear. There would be one that went to Pune to Dhruvi, and a couple to our friends' children. He would send off one to Shruti too, wherever she was, completely ignoring her sneering stance about 'elitist Alphonso'. He would bug her by saying she was free to eat all those misshapen north and south Indian fruit that masqueraded as mangoes, but one box of Hapus had already been dispatched to her. He would sometimes mime how she must be relishing them secretly, perhaps in the bathroom or with her head inside a cupboard, or how the toiling masses that she shared them with would be forever changed, in one bite. In later years, Shruti would wag her head in disapproval but smile and even grin, especially if her brother was around and he added some other crazy theories and scenarios.

This mango sending was a throwback to Ashwin's childhood days when elders sent crates to the young by road transport. Not for Ashwin, the modern dial-a-mango, faceless and much easier transaction. He would go himself to Crawford Market, strike a deal, address the crates or boxes in dark blue marker, and have the dealer deliver them through his own transport network. For the house, he would have one crate staying warm under the bed, the smell of hay and ripening Alphonso taking over the room. A riper lot would be sitting on top of the fridge, neatly laid out so that they didn't press and dent each other, but fitted snugly against one another.

I did not carry on his legacy. Well I do in a way, but with the less earthy options. I use a credit card and do the whole thing online. I send them only to Dhruvi. I don't force-feed Shruti any, because I simply do not have Ashwin's panache in steamrollering her in this matter. For myself, I don't buy any. At first I thought it was because it made me sad; but I recognize that it is more because, for me, mango season – buying, storing, eating – is a loud, bustly, family affair. Like buying beer. And I just don't see myself buying beer unless there's someone coming over. It seems to be the same with mangoes, in my mind. One season without Ashwin, it is quite possible that I didn't eat any at all and a couple of other seasons I must have eaten them only when they were served to me, or perhaps in some store-bought mango ice cream.

This year, there is a new mango-devotee around. Already he has eaten too many, but that seems to stop Aidan only briefly, till his stomach is okay again. Today he comes in bearing two boxes of them, one for me and one for Moni, and my flat smells of mangoes and hay again. He will soon go on to Chiplun on the coast for his INDog work, and he says he has chosen this next halt wisely, as the mangoes there will be straight from the orchards and won't have been jostled around in trucks. Not that he can taste the difference, he clarifies, but he likes the idea immensely.

He tells me that most Indian foods that he likes have made him sick for a bit and then suited him perfectly, wherever he has travelled in the country. Karipatta, he informs me, used to at first 'exit from my body intact and whole the next morning' if he had had it the previous day in his meal. Now he loves it and digests it perfectly. I am growing used to Aidan's casually graphic descriptions. They are not meant to shock or amuse or gross you out; they are just there, and it probably has something to do with his being a vet and seeing most things as bodily processes. I suppose that is one explanation. Or, as Moni has said a couple of times, maybe he's just a freak who doesn't know how to filter such information.

He has been asking about drinking bhang recently, and he pronounces it 'bung'. When I correct him, and get him to say bhaaang, he manages to get it right. But Holi has gone, and Farhan and Orup from downstairs, who access very good stuff, say that it's not easily available now, and it's not advisable to drink it out of season. Aidan is amused at all this season-related eating, and seems to take it with a big pinch of salt, seeing it as some kind of fussy Indian pre-occupation that has no real scientific basis whatsoever.

Farhan explains, 'Well if you get hold of any in the summer, and you do consume it, it doesn't do much for you in the intoxication department, and it can, err . . . constipate your severely,' he adds delicately.

To which Aidan says, 'Ah I see, so bhang can bung you up.'

I, for one, am done with that substance. I've had bhang in my college days, and I remember just sleeping a lot. Then Ashwin and I had it once, and it was heady fun. Like people describe, time and space had got fantastically altered, and I remember feeling like I was inhabiting a giant green bean, and Ashwin saying to me as we crossed the road, walking home, 'I feel as if I was born and brought up on this road. It is going on for very long, this road.' When we had finally reached home, me still inside my mind's giant green bean, he had pulled out his tabla and played it for friends who had come back with us. This is when he had got stuck inside the ten-beat cycle of a jhaptaal, and on and on he went on his tabla, speaking out the syllables: *dhi na dhi dhi na / ti na dhi dhi na.*

Someone began to sing a Hindi film song set to this ten-beat cycle: '*Awaz de ke hame tum bulao / mohabbat mein itana na hum ko satao*'. And for over an hour this went on round and round and round as if the entire world was now only ever about these words and the percussion sound *dhi na dhi dhi na/ti na dhi dhi na*. Someone began to play it on a little side-table, and it was difficult getting him to stop and go home, because his entire world too had become urgently and unwaveringly about *dhi na dhi dhi na/ti na dhi dhi na*. Finally people simply slept it off on the carpets and the sofas, and we woke up quite okay.

It was many years later, just a year or so back, that I had a close encounter with bhang, and I have sworn off it. Farhan's paper mosaic 'Ranthambore triptych' had got picked up by a private collector from the UK for a truly glorious sum of money and a crackling good review in the *Guardian* without him ever having 'worked the art critics circuit' or any of that.

Orup had thrown him a small party in someone's recently vacated apartment in Worli, overlooking the sea. He was always looking to get Farhan to rest his eyes, and he thought this horizon-view venue would be just the thing for him. It was just a little after Holi that year, and they served bhang-laced thandai to a group of six or eight of us. We had sat around in this amazingly empty apartment, with its windows down to the floor, and the complete absence of any visual distraction but the sea arching in front of us.

The whole party, if it could be called that, was the opposite of a 'treat to the senses'. It was a kind of holiday given to the senses. There was just cut fruit as starters, and lightly seasoned curd-rice for later, kept in the middle of the floor in two big steel dabbas. There were leaf-plates for the food, and clay kullads for the bhang, so that there would be no washing and no plastic waste. The setting was so minimalistic; I was fascinated to realize that, for Orup and Farhaan, a break from work means a break from colours and textures.

We sat around quietly against the white walls, drinking the thandai, which was very flavourful, but didn't seem to be hitting anyone. We drank plenty of it, slowly but surely, ladling it out of the big steel milk can in which it had been brought. We must have been there almost two hours, and the other people who were there declared the thandai 'tasty but not at all potent'. It was getting late, and we ate up the chaste curd-rice and left. There was some joking about 'drive safe' etc, but we were all quite disappointed at the absence of nasha. (All of this was a year or so before the cops got really strict about drunk driving.)

I was driving, with Orup and Farhan having piled in at the back, and the steel dabbas in the front. I was perfectly alright, till what must have been the last half-kilometre near home. And then, without any sort of warning, the road in front of me turned into a giant screen. And a vivid and horrible film seemed to be projected on it. I could not take my eyes off the visuals that were coming up, but I kept driving, as if on some sort of default mode. It was a little past midnight and traffic in our area had quietened down, but some inner warning system made me veer left and park, not taking the last intersection that took us to our lane. I shut my eyes to see if the film would stop, but inside my closed eyes was quite another film. By this time the bhang had kicked in for Orup and Farhan too, and between the three of us there was only enough sense left to herd each other to our lane, then to the building gate and into our own homes.

I lay down on my bed, but that position made it all worse. The road-movie was over now, but if I shut my eyes, the inside movie was on at a crescendo. If I kept my eyes wide open, the mind-pictures stopped at once, but a feeling of great doom descended, 'Okay, I am now sentenced to live out the rest of my life with my eyes wide open and to never leave the safety of this bed.' I got up to drink some water, and was surprised to see that my step as well as my grip on the glass was firm – no lurching and no fumbling. I drank a lot of water, hoping to flush whatever it was out of my system. I had looked at the clock at 12.16 a.m. A lot of time seemed to have passed, but when I looked at the clock again, it was just 12.23.

So this is how I have to live out my life, I thought. Entire miserable lifetimes embedded in every minute. I didn't dare shut my eyes, because the film that instantly started up inside my head was so awful that now I rarely go back to those images or describe them to anyone. It was as if I was inside Ashwin's head and watching the process of dying. I seemed to be actually walking in his shoes, because when I looked down at myself, I saw the ends of his cargo pants and brown loafers beneath them – the clothes that he had died in. And I was not so much walking as being propelled at a manic speed down a neon-lit tunnel that was just about my height and width. My own private conduit to hell. If up until then I had not quite understood people's fear of death, now I was assured that this is what it would be like – that it would be terrifying and no one could tell you how long it would take, even after you were dead to your family. Maybe poor Ashwin was still transiting in his tunnel, and that's why I could see him, be him, was my next mind-numbing thought.

I waited till dawn, unable to shut my eyes, and no amount of water would flush the thing out of my system. At 7 a.m. I made a call to a doctor friend and asked her if she had had any experience of bhang, and from what seemed a land very far away, she replied something that must have been, 'Viva, it's not like booze, it's broken down into its enzyme level and has to be metabolized out of your system.' Or I may have not made that call and I only thought that I had had this conversation. Who knows? I know she had stopped herself from showing any surprise or disapproval about a person like me, nearly sixty at the time, drinking anything more than a sober vodka or a glass of beer.

It took nearly twenty-four hours for me to feel okay again. Orup and Farhan had had no bizarre moments; they had just slept it off, so

I didn't tell them much. Anyway, other people's hallucinations are almost as pointless to listen to as other people's dreams.

I tell Aidan briefly about why I will never do this bhang thing ever again, and that I am now too old for it. I tell him that the pictures that come up in my head as I fall asleep to a piece of music is the nearest that I will ever go to hallucinating again. And those are never grotesque or disturbing.

He asks me, 'If I get some of it, will you let me have it at your place, so that you can stop me if I go all witless and begin to crawl up the walls?'

I say no, I don't want any part of it. Aidan is fifty-four himself, but I stop myself from cautioning him on any age level. For people from the Western world, age really is just a number, perhaps. And out-and-out 'do this, don't do this' kind of advising injunctions are most unwelcome to them, I am guessing. In India, we dispense advice of this kind freely and welcome it too, most times.

'Ah come on . . .' he says, but before I can tell him to go find somewhere else to experiment, my phone rings and it is Shruti from Rajasthan.

Her cool restrained communication has given way to a jumble of words and sentences in a high-pitched voice that I have never heard from her: 'Mom, I had put your telephone number down on his card too, Mom, and mine, and a few others. Just to guard against this kind of thing, Mom. But the people accompanying him from Nepal, idiots, lost track of him in the crowd getting off and getting in, and they got off but he got left behind on the train, and then a policeman called, and said someone had pulled the chain to stop the train.' (Here her voice broke and she half laughed and half sobbed.) 'He's such a smart fellow, Ma, he didn't panic, he just showed them the card and they tried to call me, but I was not here, and so he is being sent to Mumbai because of your number on the card and they'll call you now, and I'm coming by night, Mom, but will you go fetch him from the railway police at Mumbai Central?'

'Who, Shruti, who? Who has my number, who is with the police? Who should I pick up from Mumbai Central?' I wish you wouldn't be so damned secretive on a regular basis is what I just stopped myself from saying. Why must you give me access to your life only in spoonfuls like this? If you've given some stranger my number, at least you should tell me who it is. But I didn't say any of this. Something big had happened, and she had come quite undone.

'Emanto, Mom. His name is Emanto. He's just turned eight.'

15

Bottle-green Cardigan

'Emanto? Imanto? Which eight-year-old? Shruti, when . . .' I was trying not to sound angry and afraid, because she sounded frantic herself.

My mind forms the question, but there is no way that it can be asked out loud: had my daughter had a love-child and not told us? Did I have a grandchild that my daughter had simply omitted to tell me about for eight years? The words ricochet around in my head, but refuse to descend to my throat and mouth.

Shruti's agitation about this child on a train and now in the custody of some policemen lifts for a few seconds, and she hears my unsaid doubts. She says impatiently, but quite kindly, 'Ma, Ma, he's not *mine-mine* . . . but he is going to be, kind-of. I'm about to get guardianship from his parents in Nepal. I met him two years ago when he was six and had a fracture that wouldn't mend, and was brought here. His father works for us at the project. His mother is going to . . .' I hear her swallowing hard. '. . . die. Ma, she's not well at all, back in Nepal.'

And while I compute that, I also ask, 'And his dad . . . is your . . .?'

Shruti hastily adds, 'I'm not into his dad or anything . . . meaning his dad and me are not . . . his dad is a carpenter here in Rajasthan and goes back to his place in Nepal just once every other year.'

'Why didn't you even mention him before, Shruti, this Emanto?'

She simply side-steps my question and says, 'Mom, I'm getting someone to speak to some high-ups in the Railway Police, so please-please go to Mumbai Central by 9 p.m., ya? And take some proof of your ID with you.' I take down the train name and number.

I was sure this child would not be handed to me so easily, given that I was his . . . what? Let's see: 'going-to-be quasi-grandma-if-my-daughter-would-let-me-call-myself-that'. Yes. That was my legal standing with this lost-and-found child. And even if they did release him to me, why would he simply come home with a strange lady?

And what would he eat? And where would he sleep? Alone in the guest room? And what language did he speak? And would he be scared and crying inconsolably? I asked her some of these questions, but she just said 'You'll figure it all out, Ma.' This was a compliment, even if she didn't consciously mean it to be one. No, I am not desperate and craven for validation and approval from Shruti, but it felt good . . . to be in such a normal zone together, she and I. 'Ma I'll be home by very early tomorrow morning, ya?'

It was closing on 6.30 in the evening. It would take me an hour to get to Mumbai Central station. I went into the second bedroom and did up the bed and aired it. I opened the small cupboard and looked at the small pile of Dhruvi's clothes that he had outgrown. I had been reluctant to give them away in my own downsizing programme, especially his first grown-boy cardigan in dark bottle green that I had knitted for him. He must have been eight or nine then, and had said firmly that he was done with blue, pink, yellow, orange and all such colours. He wanted a khaki or brown sweater, but we had all thought that it was too grim grown-up a colour, and when I got back dark bottle-green wool from a trip with Ashwin to Chandigarh, he had approved.

I called up my daughter-in-law Dharani and told her about this Emanto development. She listened quietly and in her unflappable way said, 'Good.' She then added, 'I'm glad for Shruti. And . . . and for all of us.'

'And Dhruvi . . . what will he have to say, I wonder? Though this child Emanto will stay mainly in Rajasthan, with Shru . . .'

Rishabh took the phone and simply asked, 'Is my cagey-commie sister staying, or will she vanish into the yonder with the child immediately? We'll come too, Ma, by tomorrow evening. Ma, about Dhruvi, you know we don't have to worry. We have a sthithapradnya on our hands. The Buddha himself. And he lives up to his name; he *is* the steady Pole Star.'

'But Rishu, he's hardly fourteen. Let's not take his grace and equanimity for granted. Do talk to him about this child . . . and ask him if I can give him some of his nice clothes that he outgrew.'

'I will ask him nothing of the sort. You do what you have to do, Ma. Don't worry about Dhruv, I'll just tell him about this Imant . . . Emanto.'

I wondered whether to ask Farhaan or Moni or Aidan to go with me to Mumbai Central. Or whether that would mean one more new face to deal with for the boy. I even feverishly thought of telling Gautam-Gafoor, in case I needed his help with the Railway Police, but decided against it. I did call up Moni and quickly clued her in. She gave an admiring whistle of awe and shock at Shruti's news. She offered to come along, but I really thought it best not to confuse the police or the child with too many new faces and names in the whole equation. I knew Aidan would have come along with the quivering interest and enthusiasm of a West Highland Terrier. But it really would have raised more questions about who he was, who I was, why he was there and all of that. I left the house with Dhruvi's cardigan and a bar of chocolate in my bag for the child.

When I got to Mumbai Central, the Railway Police at the station were already aware that a lost eight-year-old Nepali boy was being brought into Mumbai on a train arriving at 9 p.m., escorted by two policemen. They gave me tea and a chair to sit in and assured me that the boy would be brought to me. The officer who checked my ID proof asked me in Marathi, 'And you are boy's who?' I must have looked like I was having a hard time finding an answer, so he just supplied it himself in the form of a question, 'It's complicated?' I nodded yes. But Shruti's 'high-up contacts' must have paved the way, because he was already filling out a form, getting me to sign and carefully taking down details from my passport.

Ten minutes later, the train was announced and I got up. The policeman urged me to remain seated in the room – 'or you will get lost and we will have to look for you', he added. Was I looking that vague or dishevelled, I wondered. I took five long breaths, ran a comb through my hair, so that I felt and looked more reassuring to this child when he came in.

Through the passengers streaming down the platform, I saw the policewoman first and then the child. She was holding his bag, her hand on his shoulder. They came into the Control Room, where she brought him to the officer at the desk.

He was a grubby little prince. That is the only way that I can describe him. The railway journey had added smudges and stains to his skin and clothes, but underneath that was a neat, proportioned body, straight legs emerging from grey shorts, dark brown close-cut hair that showed a beautifully shaped head, brown eyes. The hair and eyes both had a sort of gold tint-glint. Straight small nose, ivory-cream skin, pink etched lips. He held his little frame together with great dignity. Nothing of the last twenty-four hours of confusion and fear showed at all, neither in his face, nor in his spare little body.

To add to the princely effect was a small group of what looked like his subjects, his praja. They were actually fellow passengers who had looked out for him, fed him and kept him company in the last leg of his journey. They stood huddled curiously outside the control room, smiling anxiously at him and at me.

He smiled a small smile, fixing those brandy-brown eyes on me, and then pulled something out from his shirt pocket. It was the laminated piece of card-paper on which Shruti had written various names and phone numbers for him that he was to keep on him at all times. He tapped on my name. I straightened up and saluted, and said, 'Hajir hai'. His smile widened a little, and the small crowd outside as well as the cops inside laughed. The cop who had first spoken to me passed me the form to sign, and I realized that the child's actual name was Hemant. Apparently it is pronounced without the H . . . they say it as 'Emanto in his part of the world.

The woman police constable who had accompanied him said, in a sober aside to me in Hindi, 'He is very, very lucky . . . such good-looking (she used that horrible Hindi word 'chikna') children . . . boys, girls . . . when they get left behind on a train in those parts (she pointed upwards, north) . . . don't ask what-all can become of them.' And a genuine shudder passed over her. She was not looking for a tip or anything. Her mind was rapidly moving on to other duties, as she hung up her bag and rifle and pulled out some register. But, for escorting this child from somewhere near Indore onwards and handing him over safe and sound, I pressed Rs 1,000 in her hand for herself and the other constable who had been with her in the train. She looked at the officer on duty; he indicated with his head, 'take it'.

I took Emanto's bag, and his hand, which he gave into mine with ease. We stepped out of the control room. The crowd parted slightly, and a few people touched his head, his cheeks and said 'tata, bye-bye'. He nodded courteously to them (very prince; an unconsciously princely little fellow) and fell into stride with me. I hadn't hugged him, not sure if he would like it. But in the taxi I put my arm around his shoulder, and instantly he fell asleep against me in a small heap. When we halted at my building gate, he woke up fully, and all his careful composure was back. I had not heard his voice yet.

As I opened my house door, he took off his shoes and socks outside. When I asked him to get them in, he nodded no, and indicated that they were very dirty. I asked him what he would like to eat, and he simply said 'chaamal'. His voice was soft and husky, and I was not sure if they called rice 'chaamal' in his language, or whether it was one of those words that kids sweetly mishear – chaamal for chaaval. I ran him a bucket of hot water, and laid out a tee-shirt and track pants from inside his bag on the bed. I gave him a nail brush and mimed feet and nails cleaning. He smiled and nodded. After about ten minutes, he came out smelling of soap and shampoo, and sat very still at the kitchen table, his skin almost radiating a soft gold light. He ate a plateful of dal-rice neatly with his hands, and crushed the papad into his dahi. Just like Shruti did!

I cut two mangoes from the box that Aidan had got, and watched Emanto eating one with quiet relish. I showed him his bed, and he sat on it cross-legged.

Looking around the room, he asked softly in Hindi, 'And you? Where do you sleep?'

I said, 'Right here, today,' and rolled open a sleeping bag.

He now lay down on his side and watched me gravely, this beautiful little reclining Buddha. 'When I wake up and open my eyes, Shruti-didi will be here,' he said to me and to himself. It was not a question, it was an assurance that she must have managed to convey to him on the phone through all the confusion of his getting left behind on the train and being handed to strangers.

And then he was asleep, breathing long and evenly from the stomach like a baby, brown-gold eyelashes casting a shadow on high cheekbones.

I had forgotten to give him the chocolate at the station, and I put it away in the fridge. I took out Dhruvi's bottle-green cardigan from my bag and put it back in the cupboard. Only later did it occur to me (when Shruti teased the next day, 'Err . . . chocolate yes, but why did you carry him winter woollies to the station, Ma?') that it was odd of me to have taken Dhruvi's cardigan along for this child on a warm Mumbai evening. It must have been my utter disorientation at this whole development that prompted me to think of a little boy coming from a high-altitude village in Nepal as automatically in need of a cardigan. Or perhaps it was my mind racing ahead to knit him into my family.

16

Two Princelings

By the time Shruti arrives home by early dawn, she is her collected self again. She gives me a brief hug, and goes to take a look at Emanto sleeping. She curbs her impulse to run a hand on his head I can see, and busies herself with making coffee in my kitchen and asking the watchman to go get extra milk as soon as the corner store opens, as if there has always been Emanto in our lives.

Part of me wants to hug this softer, nicer daughter of mine; ask her about what happened, and what the future is going to be about with this child . . . and part of me wants to shake her and tell her to come off her cool-collected number. 'You're a mother now, and you can say bye-bye to cool-collected forevermore,' I want to say. And then there is one part of me who also wants to say, in the same cool-collected way, that if I am to be her back-up in any form now, about this child, she has to keep me or her brother in the loop.

But I hold my tongue. I make myself remember Ashwin's 'it happened'. He used to quote someone who he had read, perhaps Osho, perhaps someone else. The answer to many questions is just that: 'It happened'. It is the reply that silences all the whys, whens, whats. When you accept just that 'it happened', it stops you from torturing yourself with prefixes like *If only, how come, why did, why didn't, when, unless* . . . or suffixes like (It happened) *because of, inspite of, even though, without, since*.

Emanto happened, I say to myself, and to Ashwin's picture on the inside of my cupboard. (This is the picture in which he is sitting on a large flat rock in mock-swamiji pose and grinning at the camera. The rising sun has surrounded Ashwin in a near-halo. It is a picture that one of the kids has taken of him on some vacation long ago. 'Haa, look, just like god-picture,' Rishabh had exclaimed to Shruti, when the prints came. Their teacher used to give them 'god-pictures' when they did well in a test – Jesus or Mother Mary or angels or cherubs and seraphim, hoisted on rays of light emerging from behind a cloud. In muted golds and blues. When they were quite a bit older too, they whispered 'god-picture' reverentially to each other, when we got them to see *Kagaz ke Phool*; this was during the famous shot in the dusty old studio – the beam of light descends, and the voice soars, '*Waqt ne kiya, kya haseen sitam*').

Rishabh arrives a few hours later with his wife and Dhruvi, and is much less circumspect with his sister than I have been. They go take a peek at the Little Reclining Buddha, who has not moved all night, it appears, from the position in which he fell asleep, and it is now almost 8 a.m. Dhruvi takes a longish look too, and then herds us all out, saying 'don't stare'.

'Okay, uncleji,' his father says.

But I refuse to treat Dhruvi as this mature stable fellow who is just expected to take the arrival of Emanto in his stride. It's not that I want to walk on eggshells around him, but I make him his favourite Deccan Queen omelette served between two slices of toast that have tomato sauce in place of butter, and I am glad that Reclining Buddha is still sleeping while we breakfast. Maybe because, this way, the fact that I am already hopelessly in love with a grandchild again will not be evident for a while.

Rishabh asks his sister some direct questions, and surprisingly gets answers and even some doubts that she voices and some advice that she seeks! He asks unabashedly about the child's mother, how much he knows about her imminent death, where he will stay, what he will call Shruti, what her legal standing will be with him. And when there's just her and him in the room, I hear him saying, 'And now keep us in the loop, moron. We are this boy's family too. Not just people to call when there's a crisis, freak.' I almost laugh out loud at the subdued assent that I hear coming from Shruti without any protest or retaliation at moron and freak.

She now takes her cup of coffee and goes into the room in which Emanto is sleeping. She has promised him on the phone, when the train confusion happened twenty-four hours before, that when his eyes open in Mumbai she will be there. Now she sits down in front of him on my sleeping bag and waits.

At the dining table, Rishabh examines Shruti's new cell phone and shows it to his wife and me in grim satisfaction. 'At last. Connectivity with the freak.'

I smile. Yes, at last. Wanting to be contactable at all times is no more an indulgence and a luxury for Shruti now. She's almost a parent; and the aloof, self-sufficient stances and postures of the last some years are fast vanishing. Much faster than when she fell ill, had the kidney transplant, and we begged her to have a cell phone.

Rishabh pokes at her phone, pads up to the bedroom, takes a close-up picture of the sleeping boy and makes it her screensaver. Dharani tells him to stop fiddling with Shruti's phone. He says, 'Relax, she won't bite anymore. We are witnessing the Taming of the Shru.'

Now Emanto is awake, bathed and following Shruti out of the bedroom. He stays by Shruti's side, and as he is introduced to people, he repeats politely, 'Rishabh uncle, Dharani aunty, Dhruv-bhai', which makes me think of an overworked stockbroker rather than my Dhruvi, so we modify it to Dhruv-dhai, which is older brother in Emanto's Nepali.

He comes up to Dhruvi's shoulder; they are both spare, with close-cropped hair. But Dhruvi is nut-brown, naturally so, and more now because of his swimming. His hair and eyes are coal-black. Emanto is pale-fair, with those brown-gold eyes and hair. I rest my eyes on this new combination in front of me. And I think of chocolate and butterscotch. Almond and cashew. Caramel and cream. Surely I am losing it, thinking of my two grandsons in food terms? Am I going to grow fangs and cackle 'all-the-better-to-eat-you-with'? Get a grip, I tell myself.

I'm horribly happy. That's what it is.

Rishabh has steamrollered Shruti into staying on for another whole day and a night, and only then returning with Emanto to Rajasthan. A lunch party is taking shape. The usual suspects are being rounded up – Moni, Aidan, Farhan and Orup, a couple of Shruti's friends. The menu is simply going to be Iqbal Sandwich and beer. Rishabh is already galloping off to buy stuff and place orders. I can see that he is very, very taken by this development too.

I ask Shruti to make Emanto his breakfast; I am keeping the Deccan Queen omelette thing just between Dhruvi and me. Our thing. She stir-fries last night's rice with some spices and places two green chillies on the side of his plate with a boiled egg. This must be their thing. He eats neatly, slowly, crunching up the chillies and leaving only the stems. Dhruvi watches him, clearly impressed. Then Rishabh rounds up the boys and they head out.

Shruti shouts out, 'Hold his hand right throughout, one of you, at all times.' And already that's too helicopter mommy-ish for Emanto, and he gives her a small reproachful look.

They are back over an hour later, with stacks of Iqbal Sandwiches, each one in its own leaf-bowl. Iqbal is long gone, but one of his descendants makes this spectacular thing, officially known as naan-sandwich.

This is how it is made, if you don't have access to the Real Thing. Makes 4 sandwiches (but you will need to scale up, because four are never enough):

Four naans – not the tandoori ones, but the flat-bread kind.

Any bhuna gosht recipe that works well, made with ¼ kg mutton, to which you add finely chopped green chillies and coriander

Any shammi kabab recipe that works well, to make 8 shammi kababs

Potato masala made from ¼ kg boiled potatoes that you chop fine and stir-fry in a generous amount of oil, red chilli powder, jeera and dhania powder and salt

Put each sandwich together individually. For this, heat a biggish iron tava and smear with oil. Place a portion of the bhuna gosht in it, break in two shammi kababs, throw in some of the masala potato, and stir them all together with a metal spatula. Take this filling off the tava on to a plate.

Now slice the naan sideways, and place both pieces face down on the same tava, mopping up some of the oil and masalas. Turn over the bottom piece, place the filling on it, and place the top part of the naan on it. Press firmly till they sort of seal together. Slide it off the tava on to a plate, and cut into four quarters with your sharp spatula. Make each sandwich in this way.

Serve with sliced lemon, onions and mint chutney, and beer of your choice.

Or move to a city that has a mohalla that makes naan sandwich on the road, every evening.

Aidan arrives with the beer and is most miffed with me that I hadn't asked him to accompany me to the station last night to fetch Emanto. Like I expected, he has come with the enthusiasm of a small West Highland Terrier or a large Border Collie, eager to meet the child and my kids and Dhruvi. 'At last, I am kosher enough to be introduced to your tribe and to sup and dine with them,' he says.

Moni is on her way. Farhaan and Orup will both come.

The boys are back from their outing. Emanto stands quietly inside the door, holding a small brown paper packet in his hand. Shruti asks him what it is, and Dhruvi has a laughing fit, doubled over on the sofa. Emanto smiles and quietly pulls out a dog collar, a rather spiffy one, all buckles and studs and a row of bells. For the dog back at Shruti's project, he explains to her; for the kokor, he says. His name is Beeswa. Because he has bees, twenty toes (two extra hind ones), rather than the usual eighteen.

But Dhruvi is now horizontal on the sofa, laughing and hiccupping.

It seems that when they stopped to buy the dog collar, Emanto selected carefully. Each one that he picked up, he tried on solemnly around his own neck, and moved it around this way and that to get the feel of it. Neither Rishabh nor Dhruvi nor the shopkeeper could fathom why he was doing this. And when they said it's not for you to wear, he would simply nod. Till they all thought he was quite strange, and had begun to giggle at him. A few people around the shop had begun to stare too. The shopkeeper had joked and asked if he should hand the child a mirror to see how it looked on him. This hadn't affected Emanto at all, and he had purposefully tried on about eight of them till he seemed satisfied and chose this one.

Only Aidan instantly comprehended that he must have been trying them on one by one to see if any of the metal bits and pieces, studs and bells, would scratch or hurt his dog's neck. And when Shruti explained to Emanto that all this laughing was because they thought he was planning to wear the dog collar himself, it was now Emanto's turn to throw his head back and laugh himself into a scarlet fit.

17

Wicked Plots

And then everyone was gone in various directions, up hills and down dales. Dhruvi and his parents back to Pune, Shruti and Emanto to her Rajasthan project, the artists back into their foxhole downstairs, and Aidan on to Chiplun on the coast, as much to document dogs as to eat mangoes and fish and watch the monsoon's march a little later. Moni is yet to tell me the gory details of how exactly she offloaded Chichi Shishir, for which we fix a later date.

That day's lunch party has thrown up many odd notes and microtones. Orup, unaccustomed to talking much, sits in a corner sketching faces. He has not got Emanto right, and I can see why. Like a Buddha head, the child's face looks smiling and participating from one angle, and completely detached and inscrutable from another. It's only when he talks with his husky voice and little gestures – with a soft tentative 'aaaaa' or nasal 'eyyyy' when he is looking for the right word in Hindi – that he looks like any eight year old. But in trying to capture this aspect of him, Orup's pencil has rendered him too toddler-like. He has doodled the words Imagine and Emanto and Enigma in intertwined lettering in the corner of his drawing sheet.

Orup has followed me into the kitchen and half-asked, half-said, searchingly (drunk, stoned or sober, it was hard to tell with him),

'One gets wedded to one's notions and then those notions are whisked away from you, and in their place . . . does one find Truth, or does one simply encounter more notions?'

'This "one" is who? All humans, or me, or you?' I ask him lightly. And he goes quietly back to his sketching corner.

But his question makes me wonder. If I apply it to my life, yes I had notions about where it was headed, and yes they got taken away or replaced by new ones. Perhaps that's what Truth and other such big words are about. Just notions being peeled away till the very end. I remember my own mother's last gesture when she died – a shrug. Not some death rattle, or any throe, or crying out the name of the lord, or any such big moment. Just an eloquent shrug. As if one more notion was let go of, relinquished. The whole notion of life itself.

And that's why, perhaps, as you grow older, your notions are taken from you one by one, like your teeth, so that you have nothing to chew on, and your mind is just soft gum and your thoughts are just mush and slush by the end of it. *And so perhaps it's best to stop kidding yourself that Sudoku or Bridge or Crosswords are going to stave off dementia; just do good and be really nice to people and creatures, so your deeds live on, even if you are a gibbering idiot when you're old and everyone heaves a sigh of relief when you die, much as they loved you.* This last part I found I had said out loud; there was a sudden lull in the conversation around me and there was a kind of collective 'huh?'. I left it unanswered and caught Aidan and Moni looking at me slightly amused (no doubt wondering if I was flying a bit) and a little concerned. Orup looked up and nodded as if it answered his question in some way.

Dhruvi was in my bedroom, trying to find Mangalsinh Bazaar, Emanto's village in Nepal, on Google Maps, and not being able to locate it; so he was showing him Mumbai and Pune and the part of Rajasthan where Shruti stayed. He was also trying hard to explain an aerial view to someone who had not been in a plane or in a building taller than two storeys high.

In the balcony, I could hear snatches from a conversation about the concept of *Saat Khoon Maaf*, getting away with seven murders. A Bollywood film by the name had appeared, and Aidan had asked what it meant and why the figure seven. The speculation was: was it merely a metaphoric way of saying that someone had enough charm or reason to get away with seven murders, or was there some original story behind it. My daughter-in-law Dharani, making sure that Dhruvi and Emanto were out of earshot, asked of us all, 'So who would you finish off if you actually had saat khoon maaf?'

The alacrity and clarity with which people had their list of seven ready was quite shocking. And not even written – just off the top of their heads. World figures, prominent Indians, criminals and some sicko neighbours and sadistic teachers and loathsome colleagues thrown in. A mix of people that the world was best rid of, people making lives miserable on a macro scale or at micro level. Quite a trigger-happy firing squad we were turning out to be, in answer to Dharani's question lobbed so casually at the room.

The lunch had turned into tea and tidying up, and then they were all gone. I lay down in the silence, reluctant to have any music crowd out their voices from my ears. I felt bereft suddenly. There goes one more notion – that I was quite ready to scale down my life and go live on some random hillock. I was obviously not yet prepared to wind down my party, as I had thought I was, in keeping with my advancing years and all that jazz.

Ashwin's father used to say life is a party – you could be enjoying it or hating it, but it's a party. It will end one way or another. And it's up to you as well as up to your luck whether you will be prepared to leave well in time, having enjoyed it but aware towards its latter half that you must stop eating and drinking and talking. It's best that you leave when your hosts and other guests are sorry to see you go, but happy to see you to the door, rather than stumble out, taking forever to leave, oblivious of how much you have overstayed your welcome.

I was letting my mind wander along these lines as I lay there. Then with a thud I remembered that in the last some days of excitement over Emanto, I had neglected to attend to some of the agony aunt Q&As that I was doing for my friend who was herself ghost-writing it for some celeb woman for a magazine. I willed myself to put on the computer and attend to one of them that I picked out randomly. It went this way:

I am a 24-year-old girl in love with a 33-year-old married man for the past 4 years. He says that he has a very bad marriage and is waiting to end it. However, now his wife is pregnant for the second time. When I questioned him about it he said that it was a mistake and that his wife knows about me. He has promised to marry me within a year. I don't know what to believe. What should I do?

Amazing. I have read questions like this in long-ago women's magazines in long-gone beauty parlours as a teenager. And there are people still asking them. I can't help wonder why, while the human race spends millions of dollars on avoiding pain, on some counts we simply will not develop and modify. You'd think people would learn that certain things are such well-established no-nos, guaranteed to cause hideous self-harm and are best avoided. But no. The human race upholds its right to make the same mistakes – and worse, write soppy prose, sappy poetry and syrupy film scripts about it. Well, I bashed out a reply to the girl's question; hopefully at least some people reading it in the men's magazine it would appear in, would think twice before getting into repeating the pattern of Pati, Patni aur Woe.

When I did fall asleep, I dreamt a jumble of images that came from the one time (each) that Ashwin and I had given each other a hard time about the attentions of a third person. Long stories, both. Best revisited, if at all, in the chop-and-change, Picasso-like redistribution of detail, that happens in a dream.

I wake up and it all recedes, and a much more here-and-now feeling grips me. I must caution Shruti to not simply skim over Emanto's mother's death, when it does happen. Somehow, it seemed to me that he needed to encounter it . . . not every painful detail of her suffering, but he must be prepared in some way, and know when she actually does pass away. Perhaps be taken back to the village for her rites? But shouldn't I keep my notions to myself? Perhaps Shruti as well as his father will have some course of action in mind, and I should keep out of it. Just because Shru is tamer now, I shouldn't assume that she's open to my getting into the nitty-gritty of her life with this child. But she may have not thought it all through, and I should voice my concern even at the risk of being politely fobbed, I decide.

A couple of days before Aidan leaves for Chiplun, he asks me about my tangled land deal, and whether I would like to go visit it once, and if that will help me to decide what to do about it. As usual, I have shoved it under the carpet, that whole vexed matter. There has been no contact between me and the other co-owners – my smug ex-friends. I haven't given Gautam-Gafoor's suggestion that he send a few 'boys' over to 'discuss' the matter with them any thought either, in the last some weeks.

My life seems to be opening up in new directions, and I simply must tie up this thing, one way or the other. Either turn my back on it and let it simply go as a bad investment by Ashwin, or roll up my sleeves and go the Gautam-Gafoor route. But either way, it seemed like a good idea to go take one look at the place again.

Aidan commandeers a friend's car – driving in India for him is relatively easy, because they drive on the left of the road in Scotland too. As for the many little surprises that lie in wait on the road, or spring out of nowhere, he says he is convinced that it is doing wonders for his peripheral vision and his reflexes. He suspects that soon Indians will grow compound eyes like anthropods, so that we can watch each other's crazy road antics all around us, while facing in front.

When we get to the spot, the exact location of the plot, three hours later, I stand on the slope and see the shining bend of the Nira river way down below. This is where he must have stood, Ashwin, and dreamt up our future for us when he bought his share.

Aidan stands a little way off, peering at a low old wall of stacked stones, from which a florescent green fern emerges. For the first time since I have met him, he looks like a complete 'foreigner', his one-eighth (or is it one-sixteenth) Indian ancestry completely invisible now as he reddens in the hot sun and hides his turquoise eyes behind dark glasses. I take a picture of the fern and stone, and he says quietly, sounding nostalgic and homesick for the first time, 'Ah, I could show you some verrry pretty stone-and-fern walls up where I come from.'

I pick up a bit of the soil from the plot in my hand and put it in a small paper bag. I suddenly know what I'm going to do with this whole land deal. A third option that has just struck me; and I laugh out loud.

Almost at the same time, Aidan says, 'I know what you can do to give your co-owners the heebie-jeebies.'

We couldn't be thinking of the same thing, but two wicked plans are even better than one.

18

Indeed a Gift

'PROPOSED SITE FOR RABIES RESEARCH CENTRE AND HOSPICE FOR AGEING ANIMALS,' Aidan announces in a stentorian all-caps voice, as we scramble down the sloping plot back towards the car.

I have no idea what he is talking about and what he is so pleased about. It is hot and pre-monsoon muggy, and I am feeling a bit weepy about Ashwin and this plot thing. I say slowly and a bit testily, I can hear the edge to my voice, 'Once again, in English please.'

Aidan's high spirits are not at all shrivelled by my coldness. With his hands, he gestures the outline of a giant notice board. The sun is beating down on us, but he actually shivers slightly in delight at whatever it is that he has in mind. 'Get it painted in big letters on a large board, all official looking, stick it in the mud right here, and watch your ex-friends all behave like salted slugs.'

It takes me a few seconds to understand this, but when I do, I sit down on a very large flat stone in sheer wonderment at the cleverness of it. But I have to get up in a hurry, because the stone is extremely hot and I am wearing light linen trousers. Aidan takes both my hands in his to steady me as I bounce off the stone. I grip his hands, partly to not stumble and partly to make up for my peevishness of a few seconds before.

As the implication of what he is saying dawns on me, I see that it is a rather wonderfully bizarre suggestion: that I put up a big official-looking board on my portion of the plot, declaring it a proposed site for the kind of activity that is bound to appal my co-owners, 'Rabies research and hospice'. Announcing the impending, full-on presence of dogs, disease and death! That would get the smug swines to sit up and make contact with me, even if to stop me from doing it. In terms of sheer immediate impact, Aidan's plan is much more rousing than mine.

'Not that you'll start any such activity here, but you can doggedly keep that board in place and stretch the story for quite a while. You'll have them calling you, calling the authorities, calling their own meeting about the whole thing. Basically you'll have them frothing at the mouth.'

I so loved the idea. I could just see their agitation and the grim nodding of heads, '*Viva Pradhan has really gone quite junglee.*'

Aidan holds on to my hand as we walk down to the car. 'Now Viva, what's *your* wicked plan, tell! It better be as comprehensively alarm-and-despondency spreading as mine,' Aidan says, as I turn around and look at the plot once more, perhaps for one last time.

Now the muggy heat intensifies and we can hear thunder. We hurry to the car, because the last some miles of road to this spot is just tamped-down soft red earth, which can turn into a thick river of mud if there is even a smallish downpour. There is not a soul around, were we to get stuck.

Aidan is concentrating on the bends in the road, and doesn't pursue his question about my plans for the plot. Only when we are well out of the red mud stretch does he stop the car, pull out a Gudang Garam ciggy (a new discovery for him as an occasional smoker), light up and give a sort of querying jerk of the chin towards me.

'I've made up my mind. I don't want to live here, I'm not going to get Ashwin's money back from these people, but I don't want to just give them an easy time by walking away.'

'Right.'

'And I don't want to leave it to my kids to deal with, however much it may appreciate or whatever in many years.'

'Naah, don't garland them with it,' he says.

'So I've decided. I'm going to gift my part of the land . . . whatever fuzzy title and rights that I have to it . . . to the one person who can brazen it out with those fancy-pants co-owners of mine.'

'And that person is . . .?' Aidan mimes the roll of a drum . . .

'I give you: Gautam-Gafoor Esquire!' I supply.

He goes absolutely still, and then asks in an awed voice: 'Him? The goon with the golden voice?'

I nod, 'Ya. He's an almost-lawyer, right? He can draw up whatever document he wants, by which I will gift it to him.'

'Ahh! And then you can make him your rakhi-brother, as they call it here.' Aidan had sported over eight rakhis in March from various women ranging from the lady who cleaned for him to a couple of girls from his dog documentation projects in other states.

'He's just the kind of neighbour my ex-friends will quail and blanch at having,' I say, relishing the picture that was beginning to form in my head. 'He can build a garish structure there as a vacation home and fill it with his kids and his "boys" and do whatever it is that the Gautam-Gafoors of the world do in such places,' I said.

'Practice shooting? Make premium hooch? Dancing girls?' Aidan asks, brightening at these possibilities. 'And I hope he builds a ghastly overhead water tank shaped like an airplane or some such thing, like I saw in Karnataka. You could suggest it to him.'

We get back in the car and drive on, but only after Aidan makes me promise that before the plot actually goes to Gautam-Gafoor, I will get the 'Rabies Research Institute' kind of notice board put up on the spot, just for grins. 'So that your ex-buddies will be anxious, angry and confused in quick succession,' he adds. 'And while they're worrying about rabid dogs on their premises and trying to get you to see sense and all that, the next thing they know, they'll suddenly have GG the Pit Bull in their laps.'

I loved the idea of this two-step harassment that was headed their way, and I was pretty sure that I was not doing anything that could get me into any trouble, if I played it right. I don't know if Ashwin would approve of any of this . . . or maybe he would have enjoyed the twisted joke too.

We drove on, and I dialled GG's number. I was greeted with a trilling, 'Gautam-Gafoor here, what I can do for you Pradhan-madam?'

I made an appointment with him for the following Thursday. 'If you want me to send my boys to talk to your co-owners, you can just tell on phone, Madam,' he said at first. 'I told you then also, free of charge for you, first time.'

When I said, 'No, not your boys,' he sighed and said, 'Just giving word of advice, Pradhan-madam. This pakta bhi nahi, sadta bhi nahi situation, how long you keeping your land issue like that?'

Neither ripening nor rotting . . . I liked his metaphor.

I assured him that I was coming to him with a resolution, and that I would need a different kind of help from him in making good my decision.

'Very-well,' he said, and reconfirmed my Thursday appointment.

Aidan and I are some miles from a vineyard, one that has advertised its tasting-menu and a tour of the fields and the winery itself. In the middle of rural Maharashtra.

'My treat,' Aidan says, as we park and walk into the restobar at the gate of the property. We are told brusquely by the guard that the vineyard itself is off-limits today. 'VIP visit.' We have to submit to a metal detector being passed over our bodies (as if we care enough to bump off this visiting VIP) and our cars being checked.

The restaurant buffet is open, and there are some six wines to taste in tiny goblets at first, on the house.

Aidan sips a few and murmurs, 'Acidic as heck. Do these guys make it in plastic buckets in their kitchen or something?' He is more than miffed at the vineyard and winery being closed for the VIP visit and has muttered something like 'and democracy be damned' when we are told about this.

But the beer batter-fried prawns are fantastic, and we settle down to a glass of inoffensive white wine each. They will serve a 'three-grape three-leaf' salad, which the man at the salad counter makes fresh with much fanfare. He first puts the spinach, lettuce and ruccola leaves in a salad spinner and gives it a noisy whirr.

Aidan has downed one glass and is signalling for another. 'Ah, what a bugger-all affectation, this salad spinner. D'you know, Viva, what works beautifully to dry your salad leaves perfectly so that they don't wilt?'

'Pat them with a tissue?'

'Nope, I plunge them in cold water, drain them, put them in an old pillowcase, close its mouth, and whirl it above my head like this,' and here he spun the napkin vigorously above his head. The overhead hanging light swayed violently. 'You do need a little space to do it though, enough space, say, to swing a cat.'

I find myself grinning, imagining Aidan swinging some hapless cat.

The one other man sitting at a table at the far end of the restaurant glances at us, and then looks away, out of the window, from which you can see the rolling acres of grape vines. He has an open Coke bottle and a glass with a scoop of ice cream at the bottom of it. He pours the cola carefully over the ice cream, to make a Coke-float. No wine for him.

There is soft music playing, muzak really. It is the kind that I quite enjoy (for which I have been teased by my son and a few other people, who dismiss it as elevator music). It's old Hindi film songs played on the piano (possibly electronic, now). There's one beautiful song playing after another, and I realize that this is a string of Shankar Jaikishan hits. They're not all great songs, but some are so loveably corny and innocent that they just put you in a great mood. And then there's nostalgia doing its work too.

I notice that the other person in the restobar is quietly enjoying the music. He is much younger than I, but seems to be into this kind of muzak too. He has what I would call a rural Marathi face on an urban body. He is dressed neatly, quite formal, good-quality cream shirt and pin-striped dark trousers, dark brown polished shoes; I can see khaki socks. Close-cropped, tightly curled hair, wheat complexion, a good body; he seems muscular and sort of alert, under the relaxed restobar posture.

'What's the bet that he's a Maharashtra middle-order cop, out of uniform or in plainclothes,' I lean over to Aidan and whisper. Enjoying a good lunch spread alone in the middle of nowhere, talking on his phone softly once in a while, glancing at the big silent TV screen that is showing some cricket match, or lost in the music at times. He could well be staking out the place. All sorts of tangential intelligence-gathering happens in the oddest places, I believe.

'Or then he could be someone like one of your GG's "boys" – D-company,' Aidan says, showing off his fresh knowledge of some Mumbai cops-and-robbers jargon.

'Could well be,' I agree.

When a number is played particularly well on the music system, a song I had quite forgotten, I find myself bobbing my head just very slightly and my shoulders sway a bit in rhythm. It is '*Ajnabi, tum jane pehchane se lagate ho*'. I happen to look at the lone chap and he happens to glance over at me, and he is bobbing his head too. We have a small little connect moment. An exchange of something like a very small smile. More an eye-smile than a lip-smile.

Aidan notices our little exchange, and asks me in an interested but shocked low voice, 'Are you and this guy flirting, Viva?'

I laugh out loud, and the cop/thug looks at me and looks away over the vineyard again. 'Absolutely not, Aidan, it's more like an acknowledgement of a pan-Indian bond . . . more definite and more India-evoking than any anthem. The magic of good old Hindi film music.'

Aidan nods and mumbles 'sorry' under his breath.

'Don't be,' I say.

The lone man is done with his lunch, and now he picks up his glass and walks up to the bar, sits on a stool with his big shoulders hunched over, talking to the barman and the salad guy. He really is a fit specimen, and Aidan admires him too.

When he leaves, I simply have to ask the barman in Marathi, whether the guy is a cop. The man nods 'yes'. He's in plainclothes, and has been detailed to keep an eye on anyone who enters the restobar while the VVIP and his entourage are being wined and dined inside the vineyard.

'Ah, an extra V for the VIP,' Aidan intones.

As we return to our car, we see the cop sitting in his vehicle. He has an impassive, set expression on his face now. On our way, I translate the opening lines of the *Ajnabi* song that was playing ('Stranger, haven't we met somewhere before . . . Have you ever fallen for a wayfarer . . .') and Aidan says, 'And you're telling me you and this copper were not flirting!'

'Nope, not flirting, dammit Aidan, you're just not getting it.'

'Then film music nostalgia is one big flirtathon between all Indians, that's what it is,' he says.

I guess it is.

19

A Done Deal

Aidan and Moni are with me. We sit across from Gautam-Gafoor, drinking tea from the small sterling-silver cups. His bulk is tightly packed in his chair, and he waggles his fingers in the direction of the glass door for more tea. His comes in a glass that goes inside an ornate silver half-cup with a curved handle. When he catches me looking at it, he picks it up and says lovingly to it: 'From my Russian friend. I have done a big job for him in Goa.'

I quickly quell Aidan with a look so that he doesn't ask more about which Russian and why Goa in his tireless-curiosity mode. I'm sure he will be all aquiver with interest when I tell him later that the Russian underworld has a strong presence in Goa, it is said, and they don't exactly spend their time on siestas.

GG's dulcet voice is silenced for many long minutes once he hears my proposition: that I gift the vexed piece of land to him, for him to do what he likes with it. And that, before that, we put up the Rabies Research and Rehab kind of signboard, just to get my co-owners howling in protest.

About the rabies signboard he allows himself a quick grin, his beautiful white teeth flashing briefly. It is the part about my gifting the property to him that first surprises him. Then he looks away, above our heads, and sighs. He says, not looking at me, but explaining to his man standing in the room, in Marathi, 'So that that high-class lot is stuck with people like us.'

His voice is sweet as ever, but it is a dark thought, starkly uttered. There isn't a hint of amusement in his voice or eyes.

As soon as he says this, I realize how horribly mocking and insensitive it is all beginning to sound, towards Gautam-Gafoor and his family and friends.

He lowers his gaze back to me and says coolly, 'Basically, this is what I understand: you want to disgust your high-class friends by planting me right next to them. First you will give them the fear of rabies with that board you will put up, and then the fear of dogs like us.' He uses the word 'kutarrdi' for dogs, his hand gesturing to include himself and his aide/cousin. Kuttarrdi in colloquial Marathi means something like mangy curs.

I am mortified, and Aidan and Moni have gone absolutely still at the implication of what I have offered him. Anything that I now rapidly pick through my mind to say sounds either fake or more tactless. And again the merry-go-round starts up in my head, all of us going sickeningly round and round and round on garish tin-pot horses – Ashiwn and I, and our bloody-minded ex-friends, GG and his boys . . .

I blurt out, 'No, not like that, Gautambhai-Gafoorbhai . . . It's just that many new demands there are on my life, new grandson . . . Rajasthan . . . Nepal . . . I will not use that place . . . And only you . . . or your people . . . can use it without being pushed around by the co-owners, that was my thinking in giving it to you. My own children have no need for it, and they will never be able to deal with the complicated title and papers and all that . . . And if I make a will and write my share to them or their kids, it will really be of no actual use to any of them . . . just some useless paper and having to deal with godknowswho in the future.' There, I manage to say something that does not make my gift sound like a snobbish tasteless joke. And what I say to him *is* part of the truth too.

This explanation of mine, I can see, takes some of the sting away from the earlier insinuation that he picked up on: that having him and his ilk as neighbours would be the worst thing that I could heap upon my co-owners. A sweet and ugly revenge.

His expression changes very slightly. His aide leans over to him and says something in a low voice. Whatever it is that he whispers, it causes GG to look less put out, even almost smile.

He abruptly says 'Okay'. And then he adds with a sly smile, 'Five months from now, you come – you will see what I will make there. I am asking Bobda here to draw up the gift deed. We will finish off full thing in one hour.' And without missing a beat, he adds, 'I am asking my wife to send dal-dhokli from home, and you will eat with me, you-all. If you have any work this side, you go do and return at 2 p.m. sharp. She will send it hot from Borivali, by train.'

I feel absolved. I get up and we file out quickly. There seemed to be no scope to decline, and I see that the dal-dhokli meal is by way of a handshake on our land-gift arrangement. I am more than happy (even if slightly awkward) to 'break bread' with him via authentic dal-dhokli, now that we have agreed on this land-gifting plan.

We return an hour later. Aidan buys some vet equipment for his Chiplun operations; I buy some barfi for the occasion; Moni trails along as if sleep-walking. I am unsure if she is feeling wan about Aidan's imminent exit (I've been wondering about this), or as she says, my life is moving too fast for her to keep pace!

Back at Gautam-Gafoor's office, we are led to a low-ceilinged mezzanine space that is crisply air conditioned. All it has is a small conference table and chairs. Old-fashioned soup plates are laid out in four places with round soup spoons in them. In the centre of this is a huge insulated tiffin carrier and a jam jar of ghee. In a tray are glasses of water and a massive steel ladle.

'This ladle is from my guru's house. For big-big servings,' he says, and personally ladles steaming dal-dhokli into our plates. He spoons the ghee over it, and we begin to eat his wife's sensational dish. Gautam-Gafoor eats in silence, keeping an eye on our plates, and only gesturing once to Aidan to ask whether he likes it. Aidan is looking quite set for some more.

GG breaks the silence only to randomly tell us a horrible story in his chirruping voice, 'This solid steel ladle? When I was new at my guru's house . . . I must have been fourteen . . . I was serving boiling hot kadhi to my guru and some of his heavy-duty friends, all bosses of different areas, all sitting on the floor in a row and eating. One of his friends went on staring at me. Then when I was leaving the room after serving them, that fellow asked my guru loudly "which whore's knicker has he been conceived in". So I hurled the ladle at him. His forehead broke open with the steel and his skin got burnt with the kadhi.'

'Bon appetit,' Aidan says, very softly. And Moni makes a grim face, concentrating on her plate, to stop herself from grinning.

This is how you make daal-dhokli, a la Gautam-Gafoor's Gujarati wife. Or 'Borivali Ravioli' as Aidan has dubbed the dish. To serve four people:

Knead together a heaped cup of chapatti wheat dough, spiced with turmeric, red chilli powder, some roughly crushed cumin and ajwain, salt and a little oil and water. Throw in a tablespoon of gram flour, besan, if you like, but if you're allergic to it, you can skip it.

Pressure-cook a cup of half-hour-soaked tuvar daal with salt and turmeric, along with a fistful of raw peanuts that are soaked for an hour at least.

Now make the dal like so, in a roomy thick-bottomed or non-stick pot: heat some oil for the tempering, and throw in mustard seeds, whole cumin, a nice pinch of hing (asafetida), six karipatta leaves (or not if you don't like it) and 12 petals of garlic, whole (or not, as some purists don't use garlic). Throw in the pre-cooked and nicely beaten/mashed dal, the peanuts and add water slowly, till the dal is of a flowing consistency. Add a lump of jaggery and a couple of kokums or a little bit of soaked tamarind. Add a heaped teaspoon of dhania powder and a couple of cardamoms. Bring it to a boil and then simmer.

Now flour your board and roll out the spiced dough into a chapatti; use a pizza-cutter or a shakkarpara cutter to run diagonal cuts in two directions over it, so that you have diamond-shaped squares – these are the dhoklis. Lift your board and slide these into the simmering dal. And give it a good but gentle stir. Make dhoklis out of five such chapattis, and quickly add them to the dal and stir well. Boil it all together for about 10 minutes or till the dhoklis are nicely cooked.

Serve very hot with ghee, in shallow bowls, with optional add-ons like finely chopped onion, crushed peppery papads, fine sev, coriander, or sprouts.

We eat in silence; none of Gautam-Gafoor's earlier coolness towards me remains. He is now in a completely different mode, all solicitous host. When we are done, we return, one flight of iron stairs down, to his office and the document is ready on his table. The gift deed is quite straightforward, mentioning that I am co-owner of this property. The reason for my gifting it to Gautam-Gafoor is cited as 'for many kind acts and favours done for Ms Viva Pradhan's husband, who is now deceased'. This of course is a blatant lie, which stuck sideways in my throat for a minute. Dragging Ashwin's name into this story was something I would have avoided. But then I let it go. GG explained that this made it clear that it was not in any way extorted from me, this piece of land.

Whatever.

When I sign on the document, Aidan and Moni clap awkwardly, and it sounds foolish as heck in that little room. But GG smiles and says 'thanyou thankyou' in his schoolgirl voice. His aide Bobda murmurs 'dhanyavad'. 'Bobda' means lisper in Marathi. But I haven't heard him speak, and the word dhanyavad has no lisp potential.

I take out the box of barfi and hand it to him. Then GG takes something from his drawer and slides it across the table to me. 'Token money, just for completing transaction,' is his explanation. It is a tattered Rs 10 note, put in a cellophane sleeve. It's almost not there, the note, it looks that weather-beaten and manhandled. Apparently it is from Haji Malang or Shirdi or Ajmer or some holy place like that.

We say our goodbyes, and when we are out of his lane and inside a taxi, Aidan asks to see the note sealed in cellophane. When he returns it carefully to me, he says, 'It may be all holy and all, but my guess is that canny devotees just dump unusable currency in the charity box and tell themselves that they're giving to the poor. And then another set of canny Indians running these places of worship, they carefully seal these disintegrating notes in plastic and sell them at a premium to another lot of the devout as some sanctified-by-the-gods money.' He says this with much cynical nodding of his head and much exaggerated hand actions, almost acting out all of this transaction, looking over his shoulder at us.

Moni laughs and says, 'Of course, Einstein. That's exactly what it is. Everyone knows. Doesn't take that much figuring out.'

I am surprised at her sharpness.

Alone at home I put on Kumar Gandharva singing Kabir's '*Sakhiya, wah ghar sabse nyara*'. He sings about a house that he will go to; it will be 'nyara', very different. This house will be freed from the petty postures and postulates of life, where there will be no day, no night, no sin no virtue, no truth no lies, only grace. In this house there will be only my Complete Person, he sings.

Ashwin had suggested that we name the place that we built 'Nyara'. I lie on my bed and watch the ceiling fan. I let the tears fall from the side of my eyes and into my hair.

20

The Comfort of Blazers

Aidan has left for Chiplun to set up another unit for his INDdog work, volunteer at a canine vaccination-sterilization camp, and then trawl the Konkan coast on some fishing boats. Both Moni and I have promised to go some weeks later, and Dhruvi has shown interest too.

Moni's earlier sharpness with Aidan from some days ago – and now I remember a few more instances – has got me wondering. Was it Aidan using the words 'you Indians' or 'Indians' that has got her back up? The times that he has used it, he has been spot-on about some horrible Indian trait, and I see no need to get all defensive. He has been throwing himself into all things Indian with enough brio and affection for him to be able to speak his mind on some of it that disturbs him, I felt. And then there was his one Indian ancestor, which gave him a little more right to take pot-shots at Indians.

For instance, one day he met us both after his early morning walk and said softly (a change from his usual boom) and with quite some vehemence, 'Sometimes all this talk about Karma and Existence and the Universe is just a way of doing sweet eff-all about something that's right there before your eyes. And it's you urban Indians who are more glib with this balls-all philosophy and yogic stances . . .' Both Moni and I had looked a bit shocked, and he had added for good measure, 'Head in the sand and arse in the air asana.'

I had laughed at the mashing of metaphysics and metaphors, but Moni had only said: 'Explain.'

What he proceeded to tell us, and Moni had agreed then, was a good example of apathy being passed off as lofty detachment. On his walk, he had heard the persistent soft fluttering of wings, from an overhanging branch. He had looked up to see what it was, and found that it was a small bird, caught in a kite string, suspended sideways. He guessed that it had been struggling for a while and was beginning to tire. Whatever it did, the string stayed tangled around its wing. Its mouth was gaping with fatigue and thirst. It was a little too high up for Aidan to do something on his own, and he had tried to stop some of the walkers to help him bring down the bird. The reactions he had got, he listed angrily and precisely: a) People shrank slightly from him and kept walking, their ears plugged firmly with headphones piping them their music or holy chants b) A couple of people said (and here he imitated some pompous walker), 'So many sick and hungry human beings in our country, sir, why don't you do something about that first?' c) At least three different people said words to this effect, 'Leave it all to Existence; Existence gives Life and takes Life. We should not interfere.' d) Another man told him, 'It is going to die, leave it, Sir, it will be the meal of some other bird and so it goes on, the cycle. It is all biology-ecology. The Cycle of Birth and Death.'

And the bird gasped and fluttered on feebly. Till a watchman from the jogging park came up to Aidan with a cracked and perilously shaking plastic table, climbed on and asked Aidan to hand him a huge frond fallen from a coconut tree. Aidan warned him not to thwack the bird with it, but the man deftly swung this unwieldy frond a little further down, which broke the tip of the branch, bringing down the bird with it. The bird apparently took just a few seconds to recover and flew away quickly. The man on the rickety plastic table jumped off, and Aidan and he shook hands.

'Now after this, if that bird was grabbed by some predator, I would put that to Karma and ecology, but not before,' he concluded.

And both Moni and I agreed that the reactions that he had got were standard-issue do-nothing look-away attitudes that we see around us all the time.

'And the worst bloody thing is that when so many people reacted like I was actually "interfering" in some higher process, I really did wonder for a minute if I was just being a dumb un-evolved white man, and whether I should just stomp on and out of the park and leave the bird to fucking Existence.'

Was it this sharp standing apart from 'us Indians' that had put Moni off? Or was it something quite different? With the tumult and excitement of Emanto's entry into our lives, perhaps I have missed something, and there has been some kind of build-up between Aidan and her. Positive, or negative, or ambiguous, or unrequited, or . . . something. Which then made me wonder whether I would be the spare wheel in some way, were we to go to Chiplun together.

But I will not ask her outright, not yet. I decide to get a sense of her reaction if I say that she should go on to Chiplun alone and that I couldn't make it. But all that is for later. She is to come home today, and first she has to tell me the specifics of her end game with Shishir the Chichi.

It is about to rain, and the sky is ominously dark at four in the evening. Moni has left office early, since she is what she calls a 'card-carrying member of the Mumbai flooding club'. She has been caught thrice in different monsoons in appallingly dirty and dangerous waterlogging in the city. After the last time, she has decided that she has a right to find her way to safety when *she* perceives that there is going to be a problem, and not when the weatherman or the authorities or her employer does. I thoroughly approve of this.

She comes in and I hug her tight. It's been a while since we've done this, just her and me, crisp fried kaanda-bhajjiya and a Mumbai monsoon welling around us. She has got my favourite kind – what they call 'khekda' or crab-like onion pakodas. Not the pale round ones with minced onions, but red-brown pokey tangles of them, like so many crab-legs.

From my wardrobe-culling activity I have put aside a small pile of brightly coloured shawls this time for Moni. I have retained only one, the one that my son got me from his trip to Kashmir during his school days. He couldn't decide on a colour, so he decided to get the most colourful one; it looks like the images in a kaleidoscope have poured out of it and clung to a shawl. I am going to have it framed as a kind of hanging above my bed perhaps. But no, part of my shrinking of possessions involves not acquiring large pieces of anything, and if I were to frame Rishabh's shawl, it would be a huge one. Perhaps I will use it as a sofa-throw.

I have finally given away Ashwin's suits, the last of his things that stood in my cupboard. In the last two years, I have nestled against them for a few seconds sometimes. The last few times that I caught myself doing this, I pulled away with the resolve to give them away to someone who would use them. This time, I asked Shruti if she knew anyone who could use them, and she said she would take them gladly and send them on to Nepal. It was important for me to see them go. Now I felt I had for too long kept them standing at attention in my wardrobe, waiting, not for Ashwin to ever inhabit them again, but for me to let them off the hook. When I saw them folded over, slumped in Shruti's suitcase, I felt that I had finally allowed them to go off duty as sentinels of my memories.

Moni narrates the run-up to her final showdown with Chichi with a certain dispassionateness that I am relieved to see. The morning that she had come over, full of resolve to dump him, it seemed like her anger would simply hijack her plans in some way. But now it appears that this wretch has finally passed through her digestive tract and out.

Shishir Chichi preening himself over his blemish-free family and trashing hers had finally got her to realize that she would simply never be good enough for him. 'And so I called him over for dinner, let him yammer on about his work and how his graphic work now has a fan following and people are urging him to exhibit, yada, yada yada . . . And over coffee, right when he was beginning to assume that we would proceed to my bedroom, I told him that I wouldn't be seeing him again. When he asked why, I just said, "because I realize you are a Bubble Boy".

'When he asked what that was supposed to mean, I told him to go look it up on the Net. Just that the real bubble boy was a child with an immunity-related disease and was sentenced to live in a plastic bubble to keep out the germs. But Shishir was someone who had plenty of immunity – completely unaffected by the aspirations or feelings of anyone else. Happy to smell his own fart in his own bubble.'

'Moni, you didn't actually say that? I love it, but you didn't really say it?' This had gone even better than I had imagined, the last supper with Chichi.

'Did. To which Bubble Boy rose to his full height . . .'

'. . . which you must admit was not a tall order,' I just could not help adding.

Moni giggled and said 'ten on ten' as a quick aside – which meant 'full marks' for my quip. She paused to dip her bhajiya in green chilli chutney and then in tomato sauce and crunched her way through it.

'So he rose to his full height after I said the thing about liking the smell of his own fart, and said with his lips all downwards, "See, how crude and abrasive you can be? You would simply not fit in my family."

'That's when I told him to just shut it. And that I was on to him – for all his urbanity and pomposity, he was just another heir-in-waiting who would finally marry some blah-babe that his father found him. But he would take his time doing it, and run through a few innocent-idiot bystanders like me before he did marry his mummy-papa's pasand. He had notions about himself being different, and that's why all the pretend-bohemian stuff like dallying with women like me. But finally he was going to toe the line, because his music-industry-mogul father had made it clear that he would be shown the door if he was to marry anyone that they didn't approve of.'

'How predictably yawnily disappointing, Moni,' I said, and found myself actually yawning at the pointlessness of Chichi. What a waste of space, he was. 'So ultimately he will do like they say, but till then he's indulging in . . .'

'Mind fucks with women like me,' Moni said succinctly.

Moni had gone most brittle and gutter-mouthed about Chichi. But I could see that she was not hot and bothered about him anymore. She was just enjoying rolling words like 'fart' and 'bubble boy' and 'mind fucks' around on her tongue.

Apparently Chichi's last words were, 'Do you really want me to leave, or will you end up making contrite begging phone calls to me at night?'

At this point, Moni employed the words 'Get Out'. Which she says she never thought she would use on anyone, and she felt like a woman out of a 1940s Hollywood film or like the actor Pran dismissing someone.

Some days later, he sent her a long email listing why she was not 'marriage material', and that he was advising her as 'a friend' to become more lady-like. Moni deleted the mail and blocked him. When he sent her a couple of SMS asking to meet, she asked him not to push it, because she would not hesitate to stomp down in a most unlady-like manner and embarrass him in his office, or tell his industrialist parents in Kolkata that he was chasing unsavoury women who were not likely to produce perfect heirs, or any heirs at all.

'And I guess after that he's retreated back in his bubble, farting up a storm,' Moni concludes.

I laugh till I have to get a tissue to wipe my eyes.

I decide to jump abruptly to my next question, 'What's with you and Aidan?'

Moni looks uncomfortable, and asks cautiously, 'Has he called from Chiplun yet?'

'Yes, about when we're going there, and some stuff about the dogs and what he needs me to do here,' I told her.

'That's it? Just when we are going there and some dog talk?' Moni asks in a slightly exasperated and disappointed way.

This is when I say it out loud, 'Moni, is there something developing between you and Aidan . . . I sense . . .'

She holds her head in her hands, and says, 'That idiot. Now you've got it all wrong. Ok Viva, listen: never let on that I told you, but he's been asking me for my advice . . . about you . . . he's dead keen on you, but has no idea where you stand with such things, and was planning to put it across to you before he left for Chiplun and before you went there. Didn't you have any clue, Viva?'

I laugh out loud and say, 'Oh, don't be ridiculous, you . . . as well as him.'

Moni does not even smile. She pauses only to take a pull from her tea mug, and says calmly, 'It is not ridiculous. Give it a thought, at least, Viva.'

'Mad-or-what?' I ask her, using her own favourite expression, which she often uses in a kind of hold-all/umbrella-phrase way when she's shocked, or saying a firm no, or even when she's incredulously pleased at something.

I go inside to get her the pile of shawls from my wardrobe, and wish that I had Ashwin's hanging blazers to nestle against.

21

Hemanto's Hills

A few weeks ago, I had chosen to email Shruti my thoughts about Emanto and his mother's impending death. He must go there, be with his father, pay his last respects. I had dared to go one step further and advised her not to go there herself when it happened. To remain in Rajasthan and be there fully for him when he was brought back. To use the jargon that everyone is throwing around these days, but which I felt was very valid here: Emanto needed to *encounter* his loss fully, experience *closure* and then be better able to *engage* in his new life with Shruti.

Her reply was brief, 'Agreed, and thanks, Ma.'

We had come quite a distance from Shruti's standard 'access denied' mode. She was allowing me into all sorts of terrain in her life, and being more-than-civil and grateful about it. Perhaps I could even offer to go to Nepal after the rites and take Emanto to Shruti after that? 'Watch it!' I tell myself. 'Don't build up feverish notions about your role in this.' Best to stand by for instructions.

A chorus of pre-monsoon frogs from the big empty cricket maidan across my street is in full cry. They sound like chanting priests. There were three notes that I could discern: Ni Sa Re–Ni Sa Re–NiSaRe NiSaReSa. They sit there, belching out the notes in turns, each one saying just one note. I wonder idly if there are designated Ni frogs, Sa frogs, Re frogs in this chorus.

When Dhruvi was little, about four or five, I was visiting his other grandparents' home in Coorg. The gardener was scattering pesticide powder in the flowerbeds to get rid of red ants that had appeared in huge numbers. Dhruvi was following him, watching. Then he began pointing agitatedly at something, and did not have the words to say what it was. I ran to the spot, thinking it was a snake. But it was a huge frog that had settled firmly into the earth, which the gardener had not seen. It was now covered in the pesticide powder, and was looking distinctly uncomfortable, blinking and trying to uneasily stir itself out of its little dug-out. Dhruvi stared for a few seconds and then signalled to me to turn on the garden hose. He quickly picked up the watering end, put his finger to the hose so that the water would come out as a thin spray, the way he had seen it done by the gardener, and hosed down the frog thoroughly. It was a dry season, but the frog, relieved of the burning powder from its skin and eyes and enjoying the unseasonal shower, began to sing – not croak, sing, as if the Monsoon had arrived! I remember so clearly, Dhruvi looking back over his shoulder at us, and smiling, knowing that things were alright with the frog again.

Dhruvi's other grandfather, watching this tableau, had quoted something delightedly from the Rigveda, which translated something like this,

'Thou hast poured down the rain-flood.
Thou hast made desert places fit for travel.
Thou hast made herbs grow for our enjoyment
O Parjanya: thou hast won thee praise from living creatures!'

It is Shruti on the line from Rajasthan, telling me quietly, 'She's going, Ma, Emanto's mother Baruni. Not too many days or hours left for her. His father and he have left for their village. I sent them by air up to Kathmandu. It will take them another half day, by bus and on foot, to their Mangalsinh Bazaar. And then, after the rites, someone will have to get him back here; his dad will need to stay on for the sowing season.'

I find myself recklessly breaking my own freshly made rule, 'Should I go there in a few days, Shru? I could take Dhruvi with me if he can come, the last stretch is a hard journey, I know. And then we'll all come to you, and then Dhruvi and I will come back here.'

There I go, sticking my own neck out and also volunteering Dhruvi without even checking with anyone. Surely this is me placing a firm foot in old age, where you begin to over-engage in life processes – maya – when you should be heading the other way, the way of detachment. How does that Kabir song go? 'Maya, maha-thugni hum janay, ho!' Maya, that great swindler, don't we all know her!

There is such a silence from the other end that I wonder if Shruti has actually hung up in protest at my eager meddling-volunteering. But it is the new-Shru's silence. Not a sullen one, but a touched and appreciative one that is looking for words.

She asks soberly, 'You would do that, Ma?'

'For you, a thousand times over,' I want to say, like the kid says in *The Kite Runner*. It's a phrase I loved when I read, and want to use . . . or hear someone say to me! But it would be just too unlike anything she and I have ever said to each other. I only say a much less eloquent 'Yes, Shru'. Then I add, and somehow this is easier to say, 'For Emanto, a thousand times over,' and I say it in an obviously quoting, airy kind of way, so that it doesn't come out gushy.

But the truth is that when I say the words out loud, I feel them in their fullness. For this random Nepali child who is in the process of losing his mother, and who has made a place in my daughter's flinty psyche, I would really want to do something helpful 'a thousand times over'.

'Emanto's uncles will arrange for someone to escort you for the last half-day journey. That part is hard, Ma. It's almost a mini-trek. Dhruvi will be good to take with you if Rishabh–Dharani are okay with this.'

My son and his wife say yes without a hint of hesitation. Rishabh jumps into the travel arrangements, and by the next morning he tells me that he has managed to pull some border police contact to take us in a rough-terrain vehicle for the last stretch right up to Emanto's home. Their immediate consent and Dhruvi's readiness to come, for me, is as if they have, in fact, said out loud to me, 'For you, a thousand times over!'

This thought comes to me as I am packing, and I simply have to lie down to allow this realization to wash over me. Sometimes I take my son's solid-citizen decency and his wife's uncomplicated affection so utterly for granted. I need moments like this to do that old-fashioned thing: count my blessings. Before I stretch out on my bed, I choose a late morning raga, an old recording of Nikhil Banerjee's Desi. As the notes fill the room and seem to settle on me, my things, my thoughts, I have one of those long moments that contain just about everything that is jumping around in your life. The moment is devoid of any questions and misgivings; only answers and affirmations.

Everything is moving fast, and we will leave for Kathmandu in two days, Dhruvi and I. On our way back, Shru will come to Delhi airport, where we will hand Emanto over to her. I mail Aidan to tell him about my trip, and he writes back wishing he could have gone with us deep into Nepal, but aware that we are going 'on family business'. I like that phrase. On family business.

By the time we get off the seven-hour bus ride from Kathmandu, Dhruvi and I have been on the road for over a day and a night, counting the night-halt at an airport hotel. We are both tired, but our eyes can't have enough. Dhruvi is now wearing a denim jacket over his pullover, and I notice that he has carefully stitched on (he keeps adding things to this jacket, depending on where he goes with it) a cloth badge that is the flag of Nepal. He has got another badge for Emanto too.

We are met by the rough-terrain vehicle, which has a driver and two of Emanto's young uncles in it. They are wearing rain-proof jackets, and that's why I don't notice it at first, but then I see that both the men are wearing Ashwin's blazers, which Shruti was sure would come to good use. Yes we are 'on family business' here, Dhruvi and I, in more ways than one.

One of the young men is Emanto's mother's brother. She has passed away two days ago, Baruni. We ride in silence, stopping only for tea, when one of them shows me her picture on his cell phone. She is uncommonly beautiful. She has lived only till the age of about twenty-seven or twenty-eight.

Emanto's home is a two-storey kachcha structure, sandwiched between two more such houses. There are many people in the small common yard, and Emanto is sitting amongst them on a camp-cot, with his father. He looks smaller, younger, than I remember from some months ago. His beautiful face is not in Buddha-like composure anymore. His lower lip is out, as if he may cry or has been crying. His head is shaved. He jumps off the cot and walks quickly to us when we reach, and almost formally presents us to the others, 'Aji' (the word in his language for grandmother is the same as the one in Marathi!) and 'Dhai' for Dhruvi. I hold Emanto to me, and I can feel him wrestling down a small sob. His father greets us wordlessly.

It is early evening, and a light rain and mist roll in. We are served rice, dal and aalu-tama (potatoes and bamboo shoot). Emanto is now wearing the jacket that Dhruvi has got him. I gather from people around that technically he is not to wear any new clothing or drink milk for a whole year after his mother's death. But there is a general murmur-consensus around when Dhruvi gives him the jacket – that it would be really okay for this child not to be so very austere in his mourning.

As night falls, we are shown to a warm room up a narrow staircase. There is a camp-cot for me, and Emanto's mattress is laid out next to Dhruvi's on the ground. I fall asleep to the sound of the even breathing of the boys and rain falling on rooftop tarps.

Aalu and Tama (bamboo shoots) is made like this in Emanto's village:

Heat a kadhai with a couple of tablespoons of oil, add a cup of bamboo shoots, fry for a couple of minutes and set aside.

In the same kadhai, add another couple of tablespoons of oil, half a teaspoon of cumin and two red chillies broken into pieces; let them crackle, and add one small onion minced; stir fry for a couple of minutes.

Add a tablespoon of blended whole mustard paste and fry for bit.

Throw in three potatoes peeled and cut in rounds, along with salt, turmeric and red chilli powder to taste, and fry for a minute.

Add the fried bamboo shoot and one chopped tomato and stir-fry for a couple of minutes.

Add a large cup of water, close the lid and let it cook till the potatoes are tender and the gravy turns a little thick.

Garnish with a couple of green chillies cut in slanting pieces if you like it hot, or with a sprinkling of onion stems/chives.

Eat hot with rice, or 'chamal' as Emanto calls it lovingly.

Emanto loves his rice.

22

Harvesting Butter

Emanto has said his goodbyes to his family and neighbours, and some of his grave composure is back. His family is curiously full of men, barring a couple of very old women, and now his mother Baruni too is gone. Perhaps his father will remarry. Who knows.

We converged at New Delhi airport, and an hour later, Emanto was gone with Shru. I did not want to think too far up ahead about Shru and Emanto's status, their bond, or any of the prognostications that people tend to make about unusual attachments and arrangements of this kind. These dire warnings usually run along the lines of 'these people' will take advantage of 'us' and then blackmail 'us' when they know we are emotionally attached, and before you know it the whole clan will start showing up at 'our' doorstep' and all that blah. The kind of paranoid stuff that stops people from loving and being loved back by anyone except their own immediate family of four.

Dhruvi and I return to Mumbai, and Rishabh comes for Dhruvi; early the next morning, they too are gone.

I now have the space and time to pull out that little factoid that Moni has lobbed into my mind. About Aidan having feelings for me. Moni would give me a dark look for using the word factoid, with its insinuation of spuriousness. Why, indeed, am I thinking of it as a factoid? Do I think of it as a figment of Moni's mind, or as an off-the-wall thought from Aidan's jolly little head, not to be taken seriously?

I need to take a hard look at this. Now going to Chiplun doesn't seem like such a good idea, or is it that just the naturalness and ease has gone, and that too only from my mind, now? But in its place may be something even nicer. He is fifty-four, I am sixty-two. Can I shove this fact into the age-is-just-a-number slot and then consider this thing? And what exactly is this thing that he has in mind. How would it pan out in real terms between two people in two different countries? And do I need any of this now? I have not forgotten Farhaan's kindly, if grim, advice from the time that I was dithering about agreeing to go out on a date with the bureaucrat Raghav fellow. He had said, looking over his reading glasses briefly at me, hunkered over his paper mosaic, 'Well, from what I gather, the pickings become leaner as you grow older. "Leaner *and* meaner",' he had added. And Moni's experiences out there were getting leaner and meaner even in her forties. But then do I really want to be 'out there' at all?

Late that evening, Aidan calls, not so much to ask me when I will travel there, but to tell me that he is on a dhow in the Dabhol harbour and they have caught 'frigging giant crabs by moonlight' and are headed out beyond the harbour for fish. 'Ah Viva, I can catch you some of the moonlight on water too if you like,' he shouts, and a potentially romantic image sounds like he is selling me fish loudly. After our call is done, he sends me three MMS of water bathed in moonlight, coloured flags on the dinghy or dhow, whatever it is called; and the third MMS is one of his skipper, the tandel, holding up a plastic tub with crabs in it.

While he is speaking on the phone, I can hear the whoosh of the water around him, as Aidan tells me about the meal that they will have on board – a curry made from at least eight different fish and clams that they throw in randomly from their catch. Apparently the tandel's wife packs him cooked rice and a ball of ground masala, oil and all, and he throws it into an aluminium pan on a spirit lamp and the little fish and clams go in. They always eat the small fry, the creatures that are not likely to fetch a big price at the auction back at the harbour at dawn, Aidan tells me. He is excited and happy, and then asks me when we are coming. It will have to be just Moni and me, I tell him, with Dhruvi having missed school for the Nepal trip.

While I am talking to him on the phone, I hear the insistent toot of three phone calls, one after the other, that are waiting to be answered. I tell Aidan that I will call him back, or that he should call me once he is back on land.

One of those calls was from my erstwhile friend and co-plot owner, Bharat, another one from his wife and a third one from the other johnny. Even their names are receding from my head, now that I have so neatly disentangled myself from them. Predictably, they are incandescent with outrage, but are too la-di-dah to be upfront about it. There is a hilarious suppressed rage in their voices, as I dutifully return each one's call. They are obviously sitting together, probably sticking pins in a little black doll that they named Viva. I am loving it. From their constipated splutterings I gather that Gautam-Gafoor has put up the Rabies Research Institute board on the plot. He hasn't yet shown his full hand – that he now owns my part of the land.

I am now so far away from them and the moment in which Ashwin has trustingly teamed up with them that I am not at all hot and bothered anymore. I am all sweet and deliciously vague on the phone. I do a word-waltz with them, first asking them why it would be a problem, then asking them if they plan to build and stay there soon, and telling them that the research facility will be in collaboration with a Swedish charitable trust (this, just off the top of my head). And then I quicken the pace to a brisk foxtrot by giving them the name and number of Gautam-Gafoor, who will now be looking after this whole thing. There is an eloquent silence at the name. Not that they may have heard of him, but their suspicions are definitely aroused.

'And he is your . . .?' one of them asks.

'Rakhi brother . . . from childhood,' I supply, smoothly and recklessly.

I will wait for the day, not too far away I am guessing, when they offer to buy me out at last. And *then* I can tell them that it is not mine to sell. That I am no longer one of the co-owners of the plot. And the best of this will be saved up for the last: the day that they realize that this dreaded Rabies Research facility is not what will be built there; what will come up is a facility that houses some seriously wicked curs of the human kind.

As I stretch out on my bed, I wonder if all of this is going to come back to bite me, but my doubt is gently pushed aside by the image, as I drift into sleep, of Gautam-Gafoor sitting implacably, unruffled, in his swivel chair, with Bobda in attendance.

I wake up with a clear head in the morning. From the fridge I pull out the milk cream that has accumulated in my ceramic jar, to which I have been adding a little yoghurt every few days. It has been lying unattended in the fridge while I was away in Nepal. I put in my little electric hand-held churner, and in a few whirrs the pure white butter separates, rising beautifully to the surface. Poetry in motion for me. I have loved it right since childhood when grannies and aunties and cooks did this with the little wood churner, and then placed a velvet lump of butter on my palm to gobble up. I gently gather the butter with my fingers, put it in a bowl, run water lightly over it to 'wash' it, as I have seen generations before me do it. I put it away in a glass jar to take with me to Chiplun for Aidan. He has become a great devotee of white butter in India. I will buy the hard chakli that he likes, and he can eat one with the other.

I set aside a glass of the buttermilk for the cleaning woman. The rest I will take down to the dhobi's dog, whose mange is on the mend – Aidan says that buttermilk works magic on the coat. And a little of it will go into the karipatta plant near the gate that needs bribing and coaxing and for some odd reason a shot of buttermilk, I am told. Earlier, Farhaan has, on someone's recommendation, regularly fed it diluted stale beer, leftover in glasses and bottles from the previous night. The parijataka next to it promptly burgeoned and flowered obligingly on this diet, but the karipatta has received the beer with stony indifference. Perhaps the buttermilk will be better accepted.

At 6.50 a.m., it is Aidan on the phone again. He is back in his little clinic-house after the night's fishing trip and the dawn auction at the pier. Now he wants to know, 'seriously Viva', when I will go there for work as well as to enjoy the place and to tell him about Nepal and Emanto. He betrays absolutely no sign that he has anything special to tell or ask. I fix up to be there in a couple of days, along with Moni.

'I think the artists downstairs want to come to Chiplun too,' he says.

Farhan and Orup? I cannot see them leaving their very Mumbai existence. They only ever go out for art supplies, gallery meetings and a drink or a meal once in a while. And when did they and Aidan get on such buddy terms, especially speech-averse Orup? I find that I am smiling to myself.

The word 'jagan-mitra' pops up in my head. That's what my dad would have called Aidan. Someone who gets along with just about the whole world.

23

Trains, Planes and Autorickshaws

The glued-to-Mumbai artists from downstairs actually do make it to Chiplun, a day after I reach. Moni decides to come with them, and does not travel with me. I tell her to stop being coy and subtle, but she refuses to be drawn into any kidding-flippant reference to what she has told me about Aidan.

Before leaving by the noon train, I prepare to send off a bunch of dog pictures and notes to Aidan. My computer, however, seems to be aware of my current preoccupations. In the last some days, whenever I mail someone and want to attach a picture, the computer jumps straight to the directory with my eight Nepal photos. My favourite is one of both boys outside Emanto's home with the lowering dove-grey sky laden with rain behind them. They are both in their denim jackets, the Nepal flag cloth badges prominent on their upper sleeves. I have sent one of these pictures, where you can see their faces clearly – Dhruvi's eyes coal black and Emanto's brandy brown – to Shruti and Rishabh and the artists below and Moni and a few other people. My computer seems to think that I will henceforth always be only ever sending this picture when I ask it to attach a file.

I reach Chiplun station in the late afternoon; Aidan has kept an autorickshaw waiting at the station. He reaches for my bag and makes as if to hug me, but changes his mind – either because you don't hug in small-town India, or because his unasked question comes archly in the way.

His clinic-project is not in the main town, but an extremely bumpy and pretty six kilometres towards the Konkan coast. It is inside the compound of an old wada that is not in use. His working and living quarters are in the outhouse of the original wada. A stand of supari palms sways behind the main house. A well and some coconut trees can be seen on the far side in front of the house; or perhaps that was the back of the house.

Aidan has already been filled in, by kids as well as other people coming by, about the exact number of resident ghosts in the wada and their various proclivities. From what he has gathered in a mix of English, Marathi and Hindi, they are the usual suspects, these wraiths: weeping woman in white; small girl in a frock with staring eyes that never close; assorted wailing unborn babies; fishermen who went out to sea and never returned; an unwed mother, still hiding from some long-ago moral police.

There is a more famous occasional ghost-visitor too, Aidan is told. It's King Thibaw (infamously exiled to Ratnagiri near here, all the way from Burma, up in the northeast, by the Brits). His ghost is said to wander listlessly along the coast, and sometimes along this very compound wall, Aidan tells me. The figure, people report, is always seen looking out towards the sea, hoping that the British ship that unceremoniously dumped him on an alien coast would return to take him back to his Burma. This apparition is dressed in full regalia, it is reported. 'Old Thibaw believed till the end in the Brit sense of fair play and was sure that they would realize that it had all been a big mix-up. And that it would all end in handshakes and apologies, old chap.' This part is Aidan's spin on history, no doubt. Fascinated by this character, Aidan is currently reading Sudha Shah's book about Thibaw, *The King in Exile.* He has also acquired a book on

Bahadur Shah Zafar and on Tipu Sultan's sons – prominent men that the Brits whisked off to nowhere.

Aidan tells me that local legend has it that Thibaw's ghost is never known to have tried to harm anyone, but the other ghouls and spectres do not come with any such guarantee. Someone has assured Aidan that they never hang around together, and you would see only one on any given night. They all look like people, he is told, but one of them can push you into the well, the other can draw you into her stomach and another can laugh into your ear all night long, depending on what circumstances they died in.

'So,' and this is the clincher, Aidan tells me, 'after dark, if any person approaches me, I must look at their feet. If they are fitted on backwards, "paai ultay", it is called in Marathi, then I can be very sure that it is one of Them, and I must just not talk to them.'

I can just see Aidan examining all visitors' feet closely after dusk. And the visitors wondering what this white man was doing. But apparently this feet-on-backwards is some kind of universal sign of ghostliness. And in the Konkan it is a well-accepted fact, so people flash torches on their own feet when they enter someone's compound after dark, to demonstrate clearly that they're fitted on the right way. I have an idle thought about how any ghost with feet facing the other way could walk in the forward direction, but perhaps I am getting too technical about this. That ghosts most likely glide and not walk like mere mortals would be the explanation.

While I expect that Aidan would be roaring with laughter at all of these bhoot-bulletins, he surprises me by saying, 'I don't go near that well after evening, Viva, I can tell you, and no beer for me after 8 p.m., so that I don't have to go to the loo outside in the night.' He also has his assistant (grandly called ward-boy, because there are three in-patient dogs) and his son sleep in the small veranda outside his room, I discover.

'Safety in numbers,' I intone, and laugh out loud. I settle down on my camp chair in the little veranda, with the coffee laced with brandy that Aidan makes me. He has broken into the chakli and white-butter that I have got him, and is crunching it up with great concentration. It has begun to rain, and two random dogs quietly get on to the gunny-sack of rice husk that he has made for them as beds. I glance at their paws, and announce to Aidan, 'Not ghosts, paws fitted correctly.'

He doesn't laugh, and I realize again that he is not pooh-poohing the whole ghost thing as I imagined he would.

It's turning dark, and someone comes in on a cycle with a tiffin carrier of dinner for him and me. I flash my torchlight at the person's feet surreptitiously, and Aidan frowns at me. Clearly, this is not in the kidding realm between us and for the people living here too. I quickly switch off my torch.

While the electricity is still on, Aidan shows me some of the work that he has done, his log, his tabulations, his pictures. He has yet not said a word about 'us', if there is some kind of 'us' quietly brewing in his mind.

We eat on banana leaves laid on a small table. The tiffin carrier has a hot but not fiery fish curry, a clam dish and a mound of fat-grained rice. Four pieces of jackfruit for dessert.

When we're done, Aidan lights up his Gudang Garam ciggy, and I venture a long puff. I'm no smoker, but the cinnamon-clove flavour works perfectly on top of this meal and the rain that is falling in two illuminated columns. Aidan has rigged up two strong lights facing outwards on top of the porch. 'Feels better with those big lights,' he says.

'Are you trying to scare me, Aidan? I'm pretty scare-proof. Only large bodies of water give me the heebie-jeebies. When the train to here trundled over river bridges, I sort of prayed,' I tell him.

He looks across at me and says simply, without a hint of embarrassment or humour, 'My Da, my old Da came to me some nights ago. Wasn't a dream, Viva. It was him.' I must have looked a bit incredulous, so he adds with only a bit of a smile, 'And no, he didn't have his feet on backwards, if you are going to ask.'

But I don't laugh at this.

'He died a couple of years ago, you know, Viva. And he was a good Dad. But I worried for him and he worried for me, a lot of our lives, and more towards the end. On account of my sister. I had this sister? Did I tell you? Severely brain damaged at birth; mum looked after her, then dad, I. She died three months after my dad, she was forty. And I knew he wondered what would become of her, who would look after her when we all got old, and all of that stuff. And when she died, just a little after him, I wished so damned much that he had lived to see her going . . . for that chapter to have closed, you know, in his anxious father-mind.'

'And last night I had this dream, Viva – I thought it was a dream – that my Da was stumbling in a dark movie theatre, and I just couldn't show him the way, and I was so bloody anxious for him, and then suddenly it was not a dream anymore. Here he was, right there outside the porch just beyond the arc of light. Standing there smiling, wide smile, and showing me the two-thumbs-up sign, like this. It's an A-OK kind of sign. It was not a dream. It was actually him, with this rain behind him and these crickets, and that sound of the train passing. Just smiling and giving me that sign.

'And suddenly, Viva, the sequence of who died first, who worried for whom, my parents' sadness and fear for my sister, her own difficult life . . . all of that . . . it just got over, you know? Over. Gone. Into silence and nothingness. In a place where it really really really is alright now. Not "heaven" or anything. Not with cherubs and harps and my sis and ma and dad gambolling in grace or anything. They and their life became just non-existent in the most acceptable kind of way. And my dad's two-thumbs-up was telling me that I too must know that it's all done with. And that I never had to really worry for him, for them, or something. All of that has been taken back into itself by . . . by the Universe?' He looks at me with the question.

Aidan's turquoise eyes fill with tears, and he lets them fall. 'Ah it felt good, Viva,' he says, 'my Dad's visit.'

I get out of my chair and hug him briefly.

He abruptly hands me my pillow and sheets, and shows me my bed in the inside room. In his bed, against the other wall, a small half-grown dog had already insinuated itself, sleeping at the far corner in a tight prawn-formation. 'Kolambi is his name,' Aidan tells me. The Konkani word for prawn. He switches off the light.

I lie in my bed and hear the two veranda-sleepers talking for a while to each other and then they fall silent too. From across the room, Aidan says, 'Could we export the Indian dog to Scotland, you think, Viva? You know Canada's taking them in, in droves. It was in the papers the other day. They love them. Scottish quarantine is way more complicated, though, but the plane ride is much shorter.'

It's the usual Aidan back, I think. He has had this kind of epiphany, about his family, in this lonely place. But now he is briskly getting on with interesting projects involving canines and quarantines. But before I can respond to the INDog transporting idea, he throws me a googly ball that comes swiftly at me across the dark room, 'And would you come? To Edinburgh? Not just on holiday. To me. With me to Scotland? No quarantine required,' he adds. Again, before I can reply, he says, 'We can live here, there, everywhere. Should we give it a shot?'

I say nothing, but only for a few seconds; then I sit up in my bed, and say, 'Yes.'

I can see he has sat up on his bed at his end of the room, and his face is illuminated by the ghostly light of his phone. It looks like he is sending an SMS.

He mumbles an explanation, 'I told Moni and the artists that if it was a yes then they should come here tomorrow to celebrate; and that if it was no, they should come anyway, to cheer me up. She wanted me to tell her, as soon as I knew, what they are coming tomorrow for – for the yes or the no.'

I want to laugh, and throw a pillow at him. 'You went and told the artists too, Aidan?'

'Yes, and your son and your daughter as well, to inform them that I was going to ask you,' he says, and I detect a note of un-Aidan-like sheepishness from across the room.

By way of justification, he adds, 'Asking them was the equivalent of having a stiff drink before asking you. Dutch courage.'

24

Three-dog Night

The day before we leave Mumbai for a four-month stint in Scotland, no one gets much of a chance to be teary or pensive about the departure, because Aidan has told us all the most bizarre conversation that had in his little Konkan veterinary clinic. Apparently, he has had to dish out medical advice to some of the humans too, though he did try to tell them that he is simply not qualified to do this, and that they should go up to Chiplun for good medical aid. However, they expect some immediate help from him, and for this, he decided to stock deworming meds and dispense them after asking a few questions if an adult or a child came in with stomach complaints. Aidan's Marathi was non-existent, but his Hindi, he had imagined, was becoming quite serviceable.

Struggling to find the words to ask a person, 'Have you observed any worms in your stools?' Aidan formulated the following question: 'Bathroom mein jaanwar aata hai?' Jaanwar is big animals; he had forgotten the word 'jantu' someone had told him for smaller organisms. 'Bathroom', he had learnt, is the pan-Indian word for motions/urinating/stools etc. Like 'sandaas', which can be the place, but can also be the product and the action.

When he asked his bathroom-mein-jaanwar question, some didn't get his drift at all, but one of them applied his mind sincerely to this question and came up with, 'Haan, kabhutar ata hai.' ('Yes, pigeons come into my bathroom.')

In the few seconds that it took Aidan to realize that the man was talking about pigeons coming in through the bathroom window, he says, he had visions of an entire pigeon being passed through the digestive tract of the man. Things got worse when Aidan tried to gesture wriggly creature, and the man asked uncertainly, 'Snakes?'

The next day, when he asked his assistant, by pointing to an earthworm, what it was called in Marathi, and was told that the word was 'gandul', Aidan decided not to venture to use this word, because it sounded far too much like the Hindi cuss-word that he had heard used so freely on the streets of Mumbai.

There was so much howling laughter at every stage of this story that the watchman from my building came up and cautioned us that it was past midnight and the neighbours were complaining. My usually serene Dhruvi laughed so much that he had loud, vigorous hiccups. Potty jokes were still funny for him, I was glad to see.

Half an hour later, our taxi arrived and we left for the airport.

We are standing, Aidan, I and three of his friends, at the corner of George IV Bridge and Candlemaker Row in Edinburgh, in front of the statue of Greyfriars Bobby, the terrier that is believed to have grieved by his master's grave for fourteen years in the 1870s. One of Aidan's friends dryly explains that while it makes a great story, the real story is much simpler: stray dogs at that time hung around graveyards because visitors fed them, assuming that they were faithfully watching over their departed masters' graves. That was the unadorned explanation.

Of course I like the myth better.

Aidan declares that he is going to install a statue of the INDog in his clinic yard, on a pedestal, just like Greyfriars Bobby. It will look like an Indian Everydog. Like R.K. Laxman's Everyman, Common Man. He will get a sculptor to use the special resin that they use for eyes to look lifelike, limpid, appealing.

Amongst the bunches of friends that Aidan has made in India, one of them is an idol-maker, whose Ganesh idols have particularly kindly, twinkling and wise elephant eyes; they are not painted on, they are ceremoniously inserted, installed, those resin-eyes. Aidan has brought back to Edinburgh, from this idol-maker, a small statue of Lord Dutta with his cow and four dogs. The eyes of the human as well as animal figures have been made with the resin, especially for Aidan.

It's a blustery morning, and for the walk from Aidan's home to the statue of Greyfriars Bobby, I am wrapped up in warm clothes that I have to buy as soon as we land. My wardrobe, per force, is growing again. My careful plans to cull and shrink the trappings of existence have been snatched from me and scattered in the laughing wind. Any notions that I once had of living quietly in a tiny space in some nowhere land have been wiped out for now. The quiet part is near-impossible around Aidan and nowhere land has become everywhere land – life has strapped me firmly into a seat on the carousel that will spin me to Mumbai, Rajasthan, Nepal, Scotland and 'where-all where-all' as they say in India and Aidan loves saying.

One of my notions, when I was planning last year to quietly fade into the background, to 'go gently into that good night', was that I would learn to (relearn to) embroider, make jams and pestos, grow veggies, sketch, make little mosaic tables from broken tiles that people throw away. And then I would surface once in a while, bearing the fruits of my labour, to gift to family and friends.

Not yet, it looks like; maybe never. I will probably not get down to making these things, because one lifetime is not enough to contain all your little plans and desires. But sometimes it really is the thought and intention that counts. And geography, age and the material world are no impediment.

Except on days like the day that I get lost in Edinburgh. Geography, age and the material world all work against me on such days. I try to memorize some routes, and set out with the geography clearly in my head. Aidan shows me the road map on his iPad. But in the middle of a walk, the whole mental picture of my route changes 180 degrees, or worse, sometimes just 90 degrees. I can step into a gallery or a shop, and when I step out, immediately begin to walk in the wrong direction, which I realize slowly but surely, some minutes later. I don't panic at all, but I wish it didn't happen, this disorientation. On one such day, when I stand uncertainly on an empty street corner at twilight, fighting the impulse to call Aidan and bleat for him to come get me, I hear it first, and seconds later it appears through the low-slung mist: a horse-drawn carriage, or a 'buggy' or 'victoria' as we call it in Mumbai.

'What are you after?' a voice asks from high above. I look up, and it is a surprisingly small woman for such a robust voice. She is sitting upright in the front, the reins in her hands. When I tell her our street name, she says 'hop on' and gives me a hand. The horse shifts slightly, as I clamber on next to the woman. 'Easy, Roza,' the woman says to her horse. I hear it as 'Easy, Raja,' and I wonder if I am hallucinating, or dead, or something – because every horse that I have ever ridden as a child, on Marine Drive, or in Matheran or on Juhu Beach, was invariably named Raja. In a few minutes, or a year, or a century, I really don't know in what time and space dimension, I am standing outside Aidan's clinic gate, and Roza is clippity-clopping away, with the buggy trundling after her. I have forgotten to ask the small lady her name. We have ridden in silence. Or maybe I told her the story of my life. I just don't know.

Aidan is locking up for the night, and when I tell him about the buggy ride, he says 'You're making this up, right? There's no buggy and woman and horse in these parts.' And then he probably sees the colour drain from my face, as I point wordlessly in the direction of the receding clippity-clop, clippity-clop that I can clearly still hear, and he smiles and hugs me. 'I'm just messing with you. That's Small Agnes and her Roza. She rarely gives people rides now – says her Roza's getting old.'

The cold Edinburgh nights, Aidan calibrates not with the temperature, but as one-dog nights or two-dog-nights. In the old days, a gatekeeper or the castellan shared his bed with one dog if it got cold, with two if it got colder, drawing body heat from his furry bedfellows. There are even colder nights, Aidan tells me, but we will probably be back in India when it becomes a three-dog-night winter in Scotland. 'And even if we aren't in India then, we're equipped for winter – there's heating, and there's you, and there's me now,' he adds.

Under his big houndstooth blanket, I drift off to sleep, just outside the tiny arc of light made by his reading lamp. Then I conjure up my favourite hallucination: I take wing and fly over my friends' houses in the dark sky. I leave my hand-made gifts on their roofs and balconies and gardens (no, not down their chimneys). A tiled foot-stool, a compiled CD of Hindi songs in which each verse, intriguingly, is in a different tune, a parijataka tree in white and orange cross-stitch, a mural of pressed flowers and wood chips, a charcoal sketch of a young Nepali woman, crochet book marks and insertion laces, glass-bead curtains, knitted mufflers with paw prints on them, a frieze of Yudhishtira and his dog at the gates of heaven. Material gifts in my virtual world.

When I wake up, there are the intangible presents from my real world waiting for me.

Acknowledgements

Thank you to Swati Dandekar, Anjali Puri and Ayesha Kagal for always reading and responding. To Nilanjan Mukherjee for hours of food talk. To Aruna Alahari for cheer-leader-like enthusiasm and faith. To my sister Mini for the illustrations and the unconventional and mutually enjoyable fee-structure!

To Nadi Palshikar, Saaz Aggarwal, Dipali Taneja and other such online allies.

To Gautam Patel for reading and for lawyerly clarifications about Viva's vexed land deal. To Dhruv Kazi for one-word supportive mails, including the eloquent 'How?'

Thanks are due to my agent and friend Kanishka Gupta, for solid support and off-the-record laughs. To Ajitha G.S. of HarperCollins for the brio, promptness and editorial inputs. To the design team for the joyous cover of this edition.